# GIRL WITHOUT A HOME

(A Tara Strong Mystery—Book 2)

Rylie Dark

**Rylie Dark**

Bestselling author Rylie Dark is author of the SADIE PRICE FBI SUSPENSE THRILLER series, comprising six books (and counting); of the CARLY SEE FBI SUSPENSE THRILLER series, comprising six books (and counting); of the MIA NORTH FBI SUSPENSE THRILLER series, comprising six books (and counting); of the MORGAN STARK FBI SUSPENSE THRILLER series, comprising five books (and counting); of the HAILEY ROCK FBI SUSPENSE THRILLER series, comprising five books (and counting); of the TARA STRONG MYSTERY series, comprising five books (and counting); and of the ALEX QUINN SUSPENSE THRILLER series, comprising five books (and counting).

An avid reader and lifelong fan of the mystery and thriller genres, Rylie loves to hear from you, so please feel free to visit www.ryliedark.com to learn more and stay in touch.


ISBN: 978-1-0943-7857-2

## BOOKS BY RYLIE DARK

**ALEX QUINN SUSPENSE THRILLER**
FIRST, MURDER (Book #1)
SECOND, DEATH (Book #2)
THIRD, ENVY (Book #3)
FOURTH, LUST (Book #4)
FIFTH, WRATH (Book #5)

**TARA STRONG MYSTERY**
GIRL WITHOUT A CHANCE (Book #1)
GIRL WITHOUT A HOME (Book #2)
GIRL WITHOUT A TRACE (Book #3)
GIRL WITHOUT A NAME (Book #4)
GIRL WITHOUT A PRAYER (Book #5)

**HAILEY ROCK FBI SUSPENSE THRILLER**
BEHIND YOU (Book #1)
BESIDE YOU (Book #2)
AFTER YOU (Book #3)
WATCHING YOU (Book #4)
JUDGING YOU (Book #5)

**SADIE PRICE FBI SUSPENSE THRILLER**
ONLY MURDER (Book #1)
ONLY RAGE (Book #2)
ONLY HIS (Book #3)
ONLY ONCE (Book #4)
ONLY SPITE (Book #5)
ONLY MADNESS (Book #6)

**MIA NORTH FBI SUSPENSE THRILLER**
SEE HER RUN (Book #1)
SEE HER HIDE (Book #2)
SEE HER SCREAM (Book #3)
SEE HER VANISH (Book #4)
SEE HER GONE (Book #5)

SEE HER DEAD (Book #6)

**CARLY SEE FBI SUSPENSE THRILLER**

NO WAY OUT (Book #1)
NO WAY BACK (Book #2)
NO WAY HOME (Book #3)
NO WAY LEFT (Book #4)
NO WAY UP (Book #5)
NO WAY TO DIE (Book #6)

**MORGAN STARK FBI SUSPENSE THRILLER**

TOO LATE (Book #1)
TOO CLOSE (Book #2)
TOO FAR GONE (Book #3)
TOO LOST (Book #4)
TOO BROKEN (Book #5)

# PROLOGUE

"I dare you to go inside."

David turned around and stared at his older brother, Jonny. "What?"

Jonny chuckled, a sound that annoyed David more than anything else. "You heard me. I dare you to go inside."

David looked around at the cave again. It was his own fault, really. He'd been wearing his emotions on his sleeve – not trying to hide the fact that the cave seriously creeped him out. He blew out a breath through his nose.

"Go on," Jonny baited him. "Are you too chicken?"

"I'm not five anymore," David snapped. "That's not going to work on me."

"Right, right," Jonny chuckled. "I forgot. You're fifteen. Such a big man. Is that why you're scared of a stupid cave?"

David glared at him. This was so stupid. There was no way he was going inside just because Jonny was pushing him to. "Shut up, Jonny. You go in there if you're so brave."

Jonny laughed. "I'm not the one standing there shaking and wanting his mommy. I didn't know you were still scared of the dark."

David clenched his hands into fists. "I'm not scared of the dark anymore."

"Oh, really?" Jonny taunted him. "So, you're not going to run home and wet the bed like you used to whenever Mom turned the lights off?"

That did it. David let out a growl and shrugged his backpack off his shoulders, slinging it to the ground. It rested on the faint trail that was left for hikers to climb the mountain – the trail they were supposed to be walking up. Stupid Jonny suggested they take a stupid rest next to the stupid cave. "Fine," he snapped. "Watch this."

And he stepped forward into the cave, even though his legs were shaking as he did it.

The cave entrance was low, but just the right height for him to walk through with the barest stoop of his neck. The rock formations crowded inward in such a way that barely any light penetrated more than a few feet inside. There was probably a bear or something living in here and he was about to get mauled to death just to prove a point to his stupid brother. David walked until he couldn't see the ground properly in front of him, the narrow sliver of light from the entrance disappearing as his own form blocked it, and then took a breath.

One more step, and the darkness would swallow him whole.

"It's okay if you're scared," Jonny called out behind him. "I'll call Mom and tell her to come up here so she can hold your hand!"

David gritted his teeth and took another step forward.

It was truly dark now, so dark that he couldn't see a thing. A short while here and his eyes would adjust, but he didn't want to hesitate and have Jonny think he was losing his nerve. Besides, maybe there wasn't a bear in here. Maybe it was something cool, like ancient cave paintings or a stash of bandit gold or just, like, really cool rocks. David took three more determined steps forward, and –

Something caught his foot, making him tumble to the ground. He gave a sharp yell as he went down, clattering onto a surface scattered with loose rocks. His knee went down heavy on the flat, hard, stone surface, and he cursed and grabbed it, feeling the wetness of fresh blood under his hand. Great. Now he'd cut his knee.

"Davey?" Jonny called out. "What happened?"

He sounded worried now, the big jerk. Served him right. David had half a mind to drag it out and make him worry, but his knee was really hurting. "I tripped over a rock, or something," he shouted back. They were probably going to have to go right home. What a stupid waste of a hike.

He squinted in the darkness, trying to see the damage to his knee. His eyes were starting to adjust well, but all he could make out was the dark line of blood – not how deep or how bad the cut was. It stung something awful. He needed to check it out in the light. He cast around, not wanting to trip over the same thing twice, searching for the loose stone or ledge that had tripped him.

He froze.

There was a large shape right next to him. Something unmoving and dark, something he couldn't really make out fully in the gloom. But it wasn't a rock. It didn't have the sharp or flat edges of a rock.

It looked…

David leaned forward, squinting, willing his eyes to adjust to the light.

"Oh, God," he said, and then he screamed. "Jonny! Help!"

"What?" Jonny demanded, his body blocking the rest of the light from outside the entrance of the cave. David was plunged into near-total darkness, which was even worse than before. “Davey, where are you? What is it?”

“There’s…” David swallowed, gathering the last of his courage to respond. “Jonny – there’s a dead woman in here!”

# CHAPTER ONE

Deputy Sheriff Tara Strong took a deep breath and flipped the file open on the table.

It was quiet down here in the records room. The one, slightly rickety table that was set in the corner of the room was small, but at least it was private. She knew none of the other nine employees of Edgar County's Sheriff's department, including the Sheriff himself, would be down here any time today. Not unless some pressing new case came up.

She had the place to herself. But at the same time, she was far from alone. The weight of memories was peering over her shoulder, sticking in her throat, making her eyes wander.

MISSING PERSON, the top line of the first piece of paper read. NAME: CASSANDRA STRONG. AGE: 15.

Tara swallowed and had to look away. She tucked her blonde hair behind her ears to keep it out of her eyes. There was dust in the air – the file and the box of evidence associated with it hadn't been disturbed in years, which, she told herself, was why her eyes were filling with tears. Simple irritation, nothing more.

Tara bit her lip and read on. The details of her sister's disappearance, ten years ago, were not new to her. She barely needed the words printed on the paper to guide her recollections. She heard the ghost of Cassie's voice in her head that night, telling her older sister she was going out. *"I'm sneaking out... Maddie's going to meet me down the block."*

Only, Tara knew how the rest of the story went. How Maddie didn't meet Cassie at all. How she'd waited in their appointed spot in her car – her brand-new car, the first one of all Cassie's friends to get one – but never saw Cassie. How the investigation purported that maybe Cassie had got the meeting place wrong, got fed up with waiting, and walked over to the lake herself – possibly going into it in the darkness, even though they dredged the lake bed and nothing was ever found.

How it must have been only five or ten minutes that she was up there by herself before Maddie turned the car in that direction anyway, and yet they never crossed paths or saw each other. How Maddie thought her friend had stood her up and the alarm wasn't raised until the next day.

How both Tara and their old sister Jessy had been so devastated by the loss that both had ended up in law enforcement, and yet neither of them had yet had the courage to reopen the case themselves.

Tara sighed and sat back from the table, leaning back in the chair, and closing her eyes for a moment. Courage was the right word. All of it hurt so much. She remembered the last time she had seen her sister, waving goodbye right before she stepped down the street, disappearing into darkness.

Tara had *known* that Cassie was going out. She had watched her leave and not said a word to their parents.

And Cassie had never come home.

She didn't know why, really, she had expected the file to yield some new and exciting secret. She was seventeen when Cassie disappeared, and heavily involved in the efforts to find her. She was interviewed by Sheriff Braddock extensively – the first time she'd ever met the man who was now her boss and mentor. She'd joined the search teams combing the area by the lake. She had petitioned him, begged him to not stop looking when it was finally called off. For months, she'd gone down there herself every day – at first to search the forest in the shadow of the Rockies, the shore of the big lake, and all the little ones beyond it, the campsites, the caves. Later, she would simply look at the lake and cry.

There was movement outside the room and Tara sniffled quickly, wiping her hands over her face, and closing the open file in front of her. The door opened just as she was getting up to put it away, hiding what she had been doing.

She didn't wanted Sheriff Braddock to know that she was looking into the case again – not yet. She didn't want to hurt him with the implied accusation that he hadn't done a good enough job, even if there was a chance it might be true. He had done too much for her in the years since.

"Tara? Are you in here?"

Tara cleared her throat as she shoved the file back into the box, smoothing down her hair one last time for good measure. "Hey, Glenn."

Her partner stepped out from around one of the shelves stacked with files. Most of the evidence boxes were pretty empty, and almost all of them were dusty. Big cases didn't happen here, for the most part.

Not except for Cassie's disappearance and the killer who had stalked the lakes region just recently. But he was gone – that case was solved.

Glenn gave her a concerned look. His soft brown eyes were harsher in the yellow light of the single overhead bulb, and his curly, messy brown hair cast shadows over his face. "What are you doing down here on your own?" he asked.

Tara shrugged. "Just a bit of housekeeping," she said. She wasn't about to mention on what case.

"Oh. Well, Sheriff wants us both," Glenn said. "We've got a case, it looks like."

Tara's eyebrows shot up, her heart pounding. Once upon a time, she had wished there would be a bit more action in their little town of Wyatt or the surrounding county. Since the last case, and with thoughts of her sister ringing in her head, she hoped it wasn't anything truly serious. "What kind of case?" she asked.

"Someone found a body," Glenn said grimly. He jerked his head in the direction of the door. "Come on. We need to head for the mountainside."

***

Tara swung her head around in all directions as Glenn parked the car beside the spot where the trail narrowed, having to maneuver carefully to fit in next to the Sheriff's vehicle and the other department car that was already there. "Who else got called in?" she asked.

"Collins and Bryant," Glenn said, naming two of the other deputies that worked alongside them. It wasn't really Tara's place to say it, and she hated to speak ill of her colleagues, but they weren't the best that the county had to offer. Collins was an older man who had been a deputy for half his life and never showed any inclination or ability to push his career further. Bryant was practically green. He'd only been involved in a few cases.

At least one thing was certain: she and Glenn were going to be the driving force behind the investigation, assuming the Sheriff didn't take it himself. Tara got out of the car with a sense of renewed urgency, needing to get to grips with the case and all the details of it.

"How far from here?" Tara asked, glancing up the trail. She couldn't see signs of anyone – not the Sheriff, not Collins or Bryant, and no witnesses. From where she was standing, she couldn't see another human being but Glenn.

Glenn adjusted his belt, pulling it up maybe half an inch on his torso, squinting ahead up the trail. "Sheriff said it's a bit of a hike," he replied. He glanced at Tara with a hint of mischief in his eyes. "You want to wait here and let us come down to you?"

Tara scoffed. "I'll be fine."

"Really," Glenn said with a grin. "If it's too far, we'll all understand."

Tara swatted at him in the air, a faux swipe that was never intended to hit him. "Come on," she said. The sun was high overhead and the August weather was as warm as ever. It was going to be an uncomfortable journey up the winding mountainside path if it was further than a ten-minute walk, which Tara suspected strongly it was.

"Did the Sheriff tell you anything else?" Tara asked, partly because she wanted more information and partly because she wanted to show off that she wasn't out of breath at all. The trail wasn't too steep, but it was necessary to watch out in order to avoid tripping over loose stones and rocks.

"No, I just got the call to come up here and came to find you as quickly as I could," Glenn said. "No ambulance, though, so I guess it's a clear-cut case. No chance of rescue."

"Or an old one," Tara said. She shaded her eyes and looked up. There was no trace of a helicopter in the sky, either. That was the other option for mountain rescue, and with the terrain so uneven here, they would most likely be hovering in the air if they were airlifting someone to the county hospital. "Maybe one of our missing persons."

"Could be," Glenn agreed from behind her. He'd fallen back naturally on the thin trail, letting her lead the way. "How many outstanding cases do we have up here?"

"I'd say four or five," Tara guessed. "I'm not totally sure. I'd have to check the records. Only a handful from the last few years that haven't been recovered."

Both of them could run through the most likely causes of death in those cases off the tops of their heads. Living in Edgar County in the shadow of the mountains, you got used to it. There were bear attacks and cougars, snake bites and those who were unfortunate enough to fall down ravines or into caves. Animal attack deaths were rare, but the injuries could compound other factors – and fear of them could push people to do strange or dangerous things, like running from bears without knowing the terrain.

Older or inexperienced hikers would overestimate their abilities and get stuck. At night it could be freezing cold at some points in the year, and the wildlife population made that even more dangerous. A lot of people who got lost or had to do an emergency campout didn't come back down. Dehydration, injury, or death from falling, cardiac arrest, lightning strikes at the higher altitudes, suicide – these were the five most common solutions to all the cases that passed through the Edgar County Sheriff's Department.

"Guess we'll find out soon enough," Glenn said. "Hey, did you speak with your sister yet?"

Tara groaned. "No," she said. Their hike was going to be just long enough for Glenn to make her feel bad about that, wasn't it?

"You should," Glenn said. "Clear the air." He was slightly out of breath. Tara glanced back to see him making his way determinedly after her, glancing up to meet her eyes when he realized she was looking.

"I don't want to," Tara said, focusing on walking again. "She's just going to start another argument." The last time she had seen her sister had been at their parents' house for family dinner. Tara made a point of going over there once a week or so, but Jessy was hardly ever there at the same time.

Only, when she was, she didn't waste any time in behaving like an ass and stirring up tension between them. Which was exactly what had happened at the last dinner, with Jessy taking every opportunity to brag about how she, as a Sheriff already, was so much better at everything than Tara was.

"If she does, then you need to take the high ground," Glenn said. "You'll feel better if you do manage to clear the air, though. It will make the next time you run into each other much more bearable."

Tara chuckled. "Only if she apologizes for underestimating me. Which there is no chance in hell she would ever do."

"Some battles can't be won," Glenn replied with a chuckle in return. He'd never met Jessy, but he'd heard enough about her from Tara to know that she wasn't the kind of person to apologize for being wrong.

"We're nearly there," Tara said, pointing up ahead. She could see someone in the far distance in a Sheriff's department uniform, a blob of khaki against the sky. It was a relief. She was already starting to feel a little thirsty under the heat of the sun, baking down on the top of her head.

"Thank God," Glenn said, echoing her thoughts. He was about an inch taller than she was, but he had a slim build, and Tara thought it was a very real possibility that she was fitter than he was. At most, they were evenly matched.

They saved their breath for the last part of the hike. When they were close enough to see that it was Bryant standing outside, keeping watch, he lifted a hand in greeting and Tara lifted hers back. As soon as they were close enough to speak, he called out to them.

"The Sheriff and Collins are inside," he said, jerking his head back over his shoulder towards a slim opening in the rock. There were two teenage boys sitting among the stones opposite him, sheltering as much as possible under the shade provided by a few strong trees that lined the trail.

"Thanks," Tara nodded. The boys must have been the witnesses who found the body. She glanced at Glenn, who nodded. There was no point in waiting. She walked right into the cave, where the Sheriff was busy setting up a light with a generator to illuminate the surprisingly large space.

And where Collins was kneeling over a body on the floor, taking pictures with a flash.

"That's not an accidental death," Tara murmured in surprise, looking down at the body of a young woman – a woman with wide staring eyes that now looked at nothing, and livid red and purple marks around her neck.

## CHAPTER TWO

Tara covered her mouth and looked away from the dead woman. She had seen a few dead bodies in her time – but only a very small number of murders. There was something shockingly visceral about seeing this woman lying on the floor of the cave, finger-shaped bruises as plain as day now that she was illuminated.

"I've called in forensics, but it looks like she's fairly recent," the Sheriff said grimly. "We're going to have to do a lot of work in situ before we can get her down the mountain."

Tara nodded. One of the big challenges that came with sprawling, nature-filled Edgar County was the terrain. Many was the time she'd been forced to wait for air support or figure out the logistics of getting someone, alive or not, down one of the mountains. "What do you want us to do in the meantime?"

"Collins is photographing the scene, and I'm going to stay in this entrance area to search for any evidence," the Sheriff said. "You and Deputy Grayson would be best suited to explore the rest of the cave, see how far back it goes and whether there's any sign of a struggle or another person back there."

Tara swallowed lightly at the idea of 'another person' – the possibility that the killer themselves could be hiding at the back of the cave, just waiting to strike. She glanced over her shoulder at Glenn, who was nodding grim agreement to the Sheriff's words. He had her back. She knew that if they got into something back there in the darkness, Glenn would be there to help.

Tara carried a flashlight on her belt as standard equipment, as did all the members of the Sheriff's department; she unclipped it and reached for her gun, not to take it out but simply to make sure it was accessible if she needed it. "Let's go," she said to Glenn, using the light the Sheriff had set up to carefully check the floor as she walked. The last thing they wanted to do was destroy any evidence.

Past the circle of artificial light, the cave plunged quickly into darkness. A small antechamber seemed to have formed at the front, near the entrance, which was where the body had been found. Away from this, however, a smaller passage ran almost straight ahead. Tara had the impression of a fault which had formed through the mountain, splitting the rocks apart down one line, perhaps the result of an earthquake or some other seismic shift.

It was wide enough to walk through comfortably – but as soon as Tara stepped forward, pointing the beam of her flashlight at the ground and walls around her to search for any visible evidence, it was like entering another world. The antechamber behind was all but forgotten. The solid rock walls pressed in, and the ceiling above only made her think of the crushing pressure of the weight of the mountain over them.

This was a place where a human could easily die, trapped, or simply crushed by falling rocks. It was a place that spoke of the power of the earth, of water that was strong and steady enough to carve through stone but was now gone.

She wouldn't ever admit it to Glenn or the Sheriff, but it was a place that frightened her.

The beam of Glenn's light flashed around as hers did, making two dizzying circles of light that never seemed to stop moving. After only a few minutes of slow and careful progress, it became disorientating. Tara paused, rubbing at her eyes.

"You alright?" Glenn asked. Normally his presence at her back was reassuring. For some reason, right now, Tara felt like she was hemmed in on five sides instead of four.

"Yeah," Tara muttered. She didn't want to speak loudly – not in here. The echoes of the Sheriff's voice quietly instructing Collins were fading away, sounds of the outside world all but gone. And if there was still someone, somewhere ahead…

Tara shone her light forward. She could only see more of the same off into the distance – tight walls, long passageway. It was going to be a long walk. She sighed and trained her eyes on the ground again. "Why don't I check the floor and the left side?" she suggested. "You do the right and the ceiling. The light flashing around all over the place is making me dizzy."

"Sure," Glenn said, his beam travelling immediately over to the right. "That makes me feel more useful back here, anyway."

Tara chuckled tightly. She appreciated his attempt at humor. It did not, however, do much to make her feel any better.

Nothing caught her eye at all; it was just jagged rock, jumping shadows, and cold air as far as she could see. There was no indication that anyone had ever walked this way, let alone done it within the last twenty-four hours.

Her flashlight beam hit space, and Tara looked up with a jolt to see she had stepped into another chamber.

"Woah," she murmured, stepping out and to the side to let Glenn out next to her. The way the thin passageway had lined up, it had been impossible to know this widened space was there until they got to it. It came out of nowhere, a complete surprise, camouflaged perfectly by the rough and jagged edges of the tunnel.

"It's huge," Glenn whispered, his voice rebounding off the walls anyway. He was looking up, pointing his beam at the ceiling. "It must have been here a long time."

Tara glanced up to see formations of mineral deposits, then ran her flashlight over the walls nearest her to see damp rock. "We're going to have to fan out and search along the edges, then make our way back towards the center," she told Glenn.

"Yeah," he said. "Yeah, sorry. I'm just… this place is awesome."

"In the literal sense," Tara said drily. She was glad someone was enjoying this incursion under the mountain.

To her, it just felt creepy.

She walked carefully along the edges of the cave, trying not to think about Edgar Allan Poe stories and horror movies and childhood nightmares. Glenn's footsteps and her own echoed together all the way up to the cave's high ceiling, another overload on her senses. By the time they had swept around the sides, met one another at the far end of the chamber, and then crossed the rest of the floor to check for clues, Tara's head was starting to ache.

"I don't see anything," Tara said at last, rejoining Glenn almost at the point where they had set off from.

"Me neither," Glenn said. He gave a short chuckle. "It feels like we could be the only humans who ever set foot in here."

"Not likely," Tara pointed out. "Hikers take that trail all the time. Our boys up there can't have been the only ones who ever felt curious to come inside."

"Good point," Glenn nodded, though the way he said it sounded like she'd burst his bubble. "Do we carry on?" He pointed his beam of light back down the way they hadn't gone yet – across the new chamber and beyond.

Tara's breath caught in her throat for a minute. She was starting to feel trapped down here, breathless. "No telling how far it goes on for," she said.

"Should we stop, then?"

Tara chewed her lip. "I'll go back and ask the Sheriff." No, that was a stupid idea – if she went back through the tunnel on her own, she'd have to cross it again to tell Glenn to come back. Unless he could hear her shouting from the other end…

"I'll come with you," Glenn said, the beams of their flashlights throwing his grin into sharp relief, casting harsh shadows over his face. "I don't want to wait alone down here."

Tara thanked him silently again for saving her without realizing it. "We'll go back together, then," she agreed easily, turning to lead the way.

At least on the journey back, the faint glow of light ahead that gradually became nearer and brighter was a reminder that they were leaving, not going deeper into the earth.

The white glare of the floodlight was almost painful to look at as they drew nearer and finally stepped back into it. Collins and the Sheriff were conferring quietly, standing at one side of the antechamber, leaving room for Lindsie Hobbs to do her job. Lindsie was the main thrust of their forensics abilities in Edgar County, a team of one with authorization to draft help if a case was ever big enough to need it. She was bending over the body with a frown, touching it gently with gloved fingers.

"Any idea how long she was here?" Tara asked, shaking her head at the Sheriff's meaningful glance.

"If people would let me do my job without asking constant questions, I might come up with some answers," Lindsie said testily.

Tara raised an eyebrow and looked at Sheriff Braddock again. He shook his own head, this time. "Tara, would you mind interviewing our witnesses?" he asked. "They weren't able to tell us much of anything when we first got here. The shock."

Tara nodded. "Yes, sir." She stepped back into what felt like blinding sunlight, silently annoyed at the fact that she was being sent to do the 'motherly' work of getting two shocked teenage boys to speak.

It probably wasn't even anything to do with that. More likely, the Sheriff trusted her ability to be gentle and calm with witnesses who needed a gentle hand. It was Jessy's voice in her head that said things like that, not Tara's own.

Deputy Bryant was still standing out there doing nothing but guarding both the cave and their witnesses, which instantly made Tara feel even worse about her uncharitable thoughts.

"What's going on in there?" Bryant asked immediately, turning to look at her with his hands hooked in his belt. It was quiet out here, but

Tara could hear birds calling in the distance, a soft breeze shaking the needles of the evergreens. She breathed in a deep breath of fresh air. The open sky was above her. Yes, this was much better.

"Not much yet," she said. She glanced back into the cave; she could hear Glenn explaining what they had found to the Sheriff, asking if he should go back further in. "Still waiting on hearing what Lindsie has to say. Other than that, we don't have a lot to go on."

"Alright," Bryant nodded. He gestured a shoulder in the direction of the two boys. "Their mom is waiting at the bottom of the trail. I spoke with her on the phone. I thought she ought to wait."

Tara nodded. "You're probably right," she said. "I'll take them down after I have a word with them."

Glenn materialized out of the cave's entrance, squinting, and blinking in the sunlight. "Sheriff says to leave it," he said. "There's no sign of anything, and with the tunnel being so tight, it's more than likely there would have been fiber or hair left behind on snags. Since we didn't see anything, his working theory is she was brought in this way."

Tara nodded. It lined up with what she had been thinking. "Alright then," she said. She shot her eyes to the side to signal Glenn what she was about to do, then turned to walk over to the two boys.

They had chosen the two largest out of a collection of rocks to sit on. Behind them, trees rose tall and strong, but behind that, a cliff edge marked the line of another drop down the mountain. They weren't too far up here, at least not compared with the peak, but it was high enough that you'd think twice before approaching that edge.

"Hi, boys," Tara said, trying to put on a voice that was more enthusiastic than she felt. She chose a rock in front of them both, sitting on it, putting herself at a slightly lower height so they wouldn't feel threatened. The older boy was solemn and serious, but the younger one still looked like he wanted to cry. "What are your names?"

"I'm Jonny, and that's Davey," the older one said.

"David," the young one snapped, almost out of habit rather than real intention. Like he was sick of his brother always using his baby nickname. Tara smiled a little. If there was one thing she could relate to, it was an annoying older sibling.

"David and Jonny," she repeated. "Can you tell me what happened earlier today? Why were you up here?"

Jonny shrugged. "Just hiking," he said. "Mom says it gets us out of the house and helps us burn off energy. I like it, too. I get to spend some time with my brother." He looked down at the last words, as if he was shy about admitting it.

David, for his part, looked faintly pleased. "Only Jonny always teases me and makes me do stuff I don't want," he blurted out, making Jonny shoot him a harsh glance.

"That's not fair," he complained. "I never make you do anything. If you don't want to, you don't have to."

"You said I was a chicken," David protested. "And – and that other stuff." His ears went red, and Tara got the impression Jonny had used some words that David didn't want to repeat in front of adults.

"Sorry," Jonny mumbled. "I didn't think…"

"David, did you go into the cave first?" Tara asked, beginning to get a grasp on what their squabble must have been about. It was the kind of thing she could imagine Jessy doing when they were around this age. Daring Tara – or Cassie – to go in someplace scary. That was before Cassie had gone. After that, risk-taking became something of a taboo for the remaining Strong girls.

"Yeah," David said. His eyes hit the ground and he sniffled, his lower lip wobbling just once. "I tripped over…"

Tara swallowed. "What did you trip over?"

David's lip wobbled much more precariously. "… her."

Tara made a mental note to inform Lindsie. If there was any post-mortem damage to the body that might have been caused by a shoe, it wouldn't give them any clues about their perpetrator. Tara softened her face, leaning forward. "It's okay, David," she said. "You didn't mean to."

David blinked rapidly, holding back tears. "Then I saw her face," he said. "Her eyes were all – white."

Tara nodded and glanced over her shoulder at Glenn. He looked as concerned as she was. They needed to keep this interview short and sweet – wrap it up to avoid any further trauma for the boys. "Did either of you move or touch anything?" she asked. "Except for when you tripped, David."

"No," Jonny said quickly. "I didn't even go in." David was also shaking his head.

"Even out here?" Tara asked. When they both shook their heads to confirm, she continued. "What about seeing anyone in the area? Maybe coming down the trail as you were coming up?"

"It was quiet today," Jonny shrugged. "We started off early. Didn't see anyone at all."

"Okay," Tara said. She was satisfied they knew nothing else that could be helpful. She got to her feet. "You boys have both been very brave. Do you want to come with me to find your mom? She's waiting for you."

David nodded eagerly and scrambled to his feet. Jonny was slower to get up, like he didn't want to show how affected he was by all of it – but Tara could tell he wanted his mom, all the same.

She knew from experience that when something awful happened, it didn't matter how far into your teenage years you were or how tough you felt. Sometimes, you just really needed your mom.

"Alright, let's go," she said. The two boys scrambled off down the trail ahead of her, leaving Tara a moment with Glenn as they walked behind them. "Hopefully, by the time we get back to the station, Lindsie will have come up with an ID."

And with that ID, they could start looking for the killer – because someone was running around her county right now who had proven they had the ability to kill, and Tara didn't want to give them the opportunity to do it again.

# CHAPTER THREE

Tara folded her arms over her chest; it was always chilly in the coroner's office, a necessity given the kinds of things Lindsie dealt with in here. Tara was trying not to keep staring at the body – at her face. Those eyes. They seemed so terrible to look at. She had the overwhelming urge to go over there and smooth her hands over the woman's eyes, close them for her – but dealing with the body was not her jurisdiction. Lindsie had left them open, and Tara wasn't going to argue with Lindsie.

"So, the bad news first of all is that I still don't know who she is," Lindsie said, addressing the room at large. Tara was standing with Glenn, Bryant, Collins, and Sheriff Braddock. Another couple of deputies had come in from the office to join them. "I've checked her fingerprints against the system and there's no match. What's more, I believe Glenn has checked our missing persons reports and not found a match there, either."

Glenn nodded confirmation. "She doesn't have a record and she hasn't been reported missing yet. But if she's local, someone will probably recognize her."

Lindsie continued without breaking her flow. "Now, the reason she hasn't been reported missing is probably because she hasn't been dead for long," she said. "I would put the time of death as being sometime in the night. Possibly between midnight and three – give or take a little wiggle room on each side."

"Can't you be more precise?" the Sheriff grumbled.

Lindsie pretended she hadn't heard him. "She was killed by… any guesses?"

"Strangulation," Bryant spoke up hopefully.

Lindsie pointed at him. "No," she said, turning to point to the back of the woman's head instead. "Blunt force trauma. It looks like in the midst of strangling her, he lifted her head and hit it hard on a rock ledge that was sticking up on the floor of the cave. He left her lying there."

"Isn't that overkill?" Glenn asked the Sheriff. "Killing her in two different ways? Does that mean he knew her personally?"

"Good FBI behavioral analysis," Sheriff Braddock said, his eyes twinkling as he teased Glenn. "Tara? Do you have any thoughts?"

Tara nodded, feeling bad for upstaging Glenn – but only a little. "It looks like his first victim to me," she said. "He didn't know how much force it would take to strangle someone. Or maybe he didn't plan this to happen at all. In the heat of the moment, he put his hands around her neck, and when she continued to try to fight him off, he raised her head and hit it on the ground to subdue her. Only, it was much more effective than expected."

"I'd say the evidence backs that up," Lindsie nodded. "It was one quick, decisive blow. Once she was dead, he didn't hit her again and again, and there was no other damage to the face or any attempt to move or pose the body."

Glenn shifted unhappily on his feet. Collins slapped him on the back with a chortle. "You'll get used to it," he said.

Glenn's face seemed to ask the question, *get used to what?*, but the Sheriff was pressing onwards. "Let's focus on getting that ID," he said. "Lindsie, you have anything else for us?"

She shook her head. "I have approximate age, height, all the usual details, if you want to circulate something."

Sheriff Braddock nodded. "That would be best. Bryant, you work with Lindsie to get an alert poster drawn up. Meanwhile -"

"Sheriff Braddock?" someone called out. All heads in the room swung to look at the door to the coroner's office; Tracy, the receptionist who covered both the Sheriff's station and this office, was standing there, trying to inch down the hem of her skirt so he wouldn't tell her off for how short it was. "Oh, there you are. I've got a call for you."

"Can it wait?" the Sheriff ground out. He was often annoyed by how Tracy disregarded most of the rules of her position – the short skirts being just one part of it – but Tara knew he would never fire her. She was popular with both the deputies and the locals, had a good head for gossip, and made an exceptional pot of coffee.

"It's your wife, and she said she needed to know what you'd want for dinner before she went to the store," Tracy supplied helpfully. She stepped forward just a bit, peering at the body, and her face fell. She covered her mouth with a quiet gasp, her eyes filling with tears. "Oh! No one warned me it was Kimmie Hutson you were bringing in!"

"Kimmie Hutson?" the Sheriff repeated. "That's who this is?"

Tracy nodded vehemently, her face paling even more as she realized she had just made the first ID on the body. She looked like she might throw up. "That's Kimmie," she said. "I'd recognize her anywhere. She's my neighbor's daughter."

Sheriff Braddock walked over to Tracy, slipping an arm around her shoulders to comfort her for a moment. "Alright. Tracy. Let's get you back to reception so I can answer that call," he said. He looked at Tara and Glenn. "Someone had better get over to the Hutson house, get a confirmed ID."

Tara nodded. "We'll go right away," she said, taking one more glance at Kimmie Hutson on Lindsie's table before she followed the Sheriff and Tracy out of the room.

***

The home where Kimmie Hutson had lived looked much like any other in the town of Wyatt. It was a family home, solid and just a little shabby around the edges, built maybe thirty or forty years ago. Looking up at it, Tara felt she could have been looking at the home where she grew up.

She looked down at the photograph they'd found on Kimmie's social media profile on the way over. The grainy, sunny shot must have been taken ten or fifteen years ago, when Kimmie was a child. She was playing on a green patch of grass, her feet dangling in a kiddie pool in the hot weather, smiling with a slightly older child – probably a sibling – in front of this very house. She had shared it on her most recent birthday.

"You alright?" Glenn asked, standing next to her on the street, looking between her face and the house as if to try and discern what she was thinking.

"Yeah," Tara said. She felt a heaviness in her chest. She hated breaking the news that a family member was dead. One blessing of the fact that a lot of their victims out in the park or the mountains were tourists was that she hardly ever needed to do this bit. They would normally end up calling a local Sheriff or other police force back in the victim's hometown to break the news to them.

This time, though, there was no backing out. No one to take the job for her. It was just one of the many difficult responsibilities she faced as a Deputy Sheriff – and would have to face as Sheriff if she did manage to take on the role after Braddock.

How did you tell someone that their daughter had been found dead in a cave?

Tara took a breath, walked up to the door, and knocked hard and decisively. She didn't want to stand out here waiting for someone to hear her. There wasn't a long pause before someone answered, a young man in his early twenties – perhaps four or five years younger than herself. The same man that had once been the other child in the photograph, Tara recognized.

"Hello?" he said, uncertainty stripping the smile from his face as he took in their uniforms.

"Hi," Tara said, feeling her heart stick in her throat. "We're looking for the residence of Kimmie Hutson."

"This is where she lives," he said. He furrowed his brow. "She's not home, though."

"We're aware of that," Tara said. She hesitated. "Can we come inside?"

He swallowed. His expression was sallow; he knew this wasn't a social call or a fun check-in. When you saw a couple of deputies on your doorstep, most of the time, it meant bad news.

"Sure," he said, stepping aside and opening the door wider.

Tara walked into the unfamiliar yet familiar house, knowing by instinct that the room where the family gathered for most of the day would be to the left. She entered a space that was dominated by two wide, long sofas with enough room for a family, oriented around a large flatscreen TV on the wall and with a coffee table in front of them. One of the sofas was already occupied by a middle-aged man and woman sitting close by one another, a football game rerun playing on the TV while they sipped mugs of coffee.

"Mr. and Mrs. Hutson?" Tara guessed.

They looked back at her with wide eyes and startled, open mouths. Tara could see their daughter in them immediately. The blonde hair and blue eyes of her mother, the thinner lips and straight nose of her father. "Yes," the father said, clutching his mug of coffee in astonishment.

The young man had followed them from the doorway. "And you, sir?" she asked. Glenn was over by the windowsill, examining something. She caught his eye and he lifted it towards her: a framed photograph of Kimmie at her high school graduation, very clearly proving to them both that the ID had been correct. That was the woman lying on Lindsie's slab. The woman they had seen in all her social media posts.

"I'm Kimmie's brother, Ryan," the man said, folding his arms across his chest. "What is this about?" There was nervousness under his voice. He knew she was dead. He had to. He was just waiting to hear them say it.

"I'm sorry to have to be the bearer of this news," Tara said, glancing around at all of them before settling on the mother. It was an instinct in her, a feeling that this was the person who most needed that eye contact. "We were called to a body up in the mountains this morning. We believe it to be Kimmie. I'm afraid she's dead."

There was a gasp in the room, a feeling like being punched in the chest and winded, all the air sucked out of you. Various noises of distress broke from all three of the family members. The brother's arms dropped from where he'd folded them over his chest; the mother dropped her coffee mug, smashing it over the hardwood floor, trails of dark liquid splashing over an accent rug.

Glenn rushed forward to scoop up the shards and get them out from underfoot before anyone stood on them. Tara watched, standing with her back straight, knowing her role here was to stay strong and answer any questions the family may direct at her as they processed the shock.

"Let me do that," Ryan muttered, trying to take over.

Glenn shook his head. "You should sit down," he said. His voice was kind. "Let us take care of this for you." His tone implied it was the least they could do, given the circumstances.

"What happened?" the father, Mr. Hutson, managed to gasp out, his voice shaking.

Tara had to bite her lip before she could continue. "We don't have the full details as our investigation is still progressing," she said. "But we do have reason to believe that foul play was involved."

"Someone killed her?" Ryan burst out. Tara glanced at him. There was a darkness in his eyes. They were going to have to watch him. He looked like the kind of victim relative that might try to get his own revenge on the killer. She made a mental note to check his record.

"I'm afraid that does appear to be the case," Tara said. "The signs point to a brief struggle, followed by a life-ending injury. I'm sorry to have to do this now, but we need to ask a few questions to see if we can bring your daughter's killer to justice as soon as possible."

Ryan and Mr. Hutson nodded. Mrs. Hutson had barely stirred, and not said a word since Tara delivered the news. Glenn had finished collecting the shards; he disappeared discreetly into the kitchen, where Tara heard the tinkling noise of ceramic pieces falling into a garbage bag.

"Do you know why she would have been up in the mountains last night, or who she was with?" Tara asked. She glanced around at three shaking heads. "Any idea why she was up on the hiking trails?"

Ryan shrugged his shoulders up and down. "That doesn't sound like Kimmie," he said. "Not on a Saturday night. She would usually go out with friends."

"Do you know who she planned to meet last night?" Tara asked, grabbing her notebook.

Ryan shook his head no. "She didn't say," he said. "We didn't keep on top of each other that much, you know? Not since we're both adults. We just come and go when we want. She didn't say anything at all about meeting someone."

"Can you think of anyone who might have been close to her, someone she might have fallen out with?" Tara asked. She thought of the physical clues, the violent struggle. Yes, it was likely the killer hadn't known her, due to the fact there had been no posing or any signs of either care or destructive rage on the body. Just one quick struggle and it was over. But that didn't mean they could rule it out so early.

"No," Mrs. Hutson said, breaking through her shock and grief enough to answer. She shook her head slowly. "Kimmie was… she was lovely."

It wasn't unusual for family members to repeat something similar. It didn't always mean the victim truly had no enemies. "What about her mental state?" Tara asked. "Do any of you recall any unusual behavior in the last week or so? Any sign that Kimmie was more distressed, anxious, or down than usual?"

Mr. Hutson cleared his throat. "Kimmie's been struggling for a while," he said. "A few years. She was diagnosed with depression. She was on medication for it, but I thought she was doing well."

"She was," Ryan confirmed. "She was coming out of it. It's been a long fight over the past years, but she was coming out of it."

"Was there something that triggered her depression?" Tara asked, zeroing in on that.

"She -" Ryan began.

"Ryan," Mr. Hutson cut him off, his voice sharp.

"They need to know," Ryan told him. He turned back to Tara. "She gave a baby up for adoption four years ago, when she was seventeen. She couldn't look after it and the father was nowhere to be found, so she made the decision, hoping the baby would have a better life. But she was conflicted about it. She spent a lot of time after that just spiraling."

Tara nodded understanding, turning it over in her mind. Could the young woman have been suicidal? But what bearing could that have? She was clearly murdered, not dead by her own hand. "In the last few weeks in particular, was her behavior different in any way?" She was thinking about bad responses to medication, about wanting to take risks that could end in her getting hurt, about falling in with the wrong people. There was still a missing piece of the puzzle, but if Kimmie's behavior had changed…

"No," Mrs. Hutson said. She looked at her other family members in turn, but neither of them contradicted her. "No, she was getting better. Looking forward to the future. There was nothing different about her."

Tara nodded again. Well, it had been worth a shot. "Thank you," she said. "If possible, I'd like you to think of a list of names, if you can, of people you know were her friends or that she spent time with. I'll have a deputy come by to sit with you – you can give the list to him. We'll keep you updated on our end as much as we can."

"Can we see her?" Mrs. Hutson asked, her voice and eyes at once full of fear and hope.

Tara hesitated. She wasn't sure if Lindsie had fully completed her work. "Not yet," she said. "But our deputy will let you know when."

She nodded at them in farewell. Glenn stepped out first into the hall, letting her have the room to leave as well, and they walked towards the door together. There was a movement behind her, and Tara looked back to see that Ryan was escorting them to the door.

She stepped outside and prepared herself for an awkward goodbye, which was always difficult with grieving family members, but Ryan stepped outside with them and closed the door behind him.

"There's something you should know," he said, the second the door was shut and the passageway back to the rest of his family was blocked.

He had Tara's attention, that was for sure. "What is it?" she asked, trying to analyze his expression. He seemed… angry, more than anything else.

"My parents didn't know, but Kimmie had a lot of problems after the baby," he said. "I mean, even more than the depression. There was a guy."

Tara's eyebrows lifted. "An ex-boyfriend?"

"Yeah," Ryan nodded, his hands clenching into fists at his sides. "He treated her really badly. When he found out about the baby, he called her all kinds of names, accused her of sleeping around. She broke up with him, but that didn't make him stop."

"What did he do?" Glenn asked softly.

"He was violent," Ryan explained. There was a flash of pure fury in his eyes. "Kimmie didn't tell me until later. He'd been hitting her when they were together. After they broke up, he hunted her down and hit her again when she said she wouldn't take him back. I took her to the police and we got a restraining order."

"This is all on record, then," Tara nodded. They hadn't had the time to really go deep into Kimmie's history before coming out here. There was clearly more to discover.

"His name is Leo Daley," Ryan said. "He's the one who did this. He has to be. He threatened her so many times. I told her a piece of paper wasn't going to be enough to hold him back, that she needed to press charges properly and send him to jail, but she didn't listen."

"We'll be sure to check him out," Tara said. She couldn't give away too much to a family member of the deceased, not without being sure. But it sounded good. Most of the time, when a woman was murdered, a current or past lover had something to do with it.

"You'd better," Ryan said. His hands were still in fists and he was shaking slightly. "Because if you don't go after him, I'm going to."

"Leave the police work to us," Glenn told him roughly. "And the justice, too."

They turned and left him, but Tara had a feeling in her gut that Ryan wasn't one to make idle threats.

They needed to speak to Leo Daley – not just because he was a good suspect, but because his own safety might depend on it.

# CHAPTER FOUR

"Is that him?" Tara asked, looking down at a photograph on the screen of her cell phone and then back up again.

"Looks like it," Glenn replied. He was squinting across her, looking out of the car window on her side. The bar had outdoor seating, and thankfully, it looked like Leo Daley had decided to take advantage of that. It made identifying him all the easier.

"Right, then," Tara said. She looked up and down the street. It was quiet today, being Sunday afternoon – a lot of places were closed, and the places that weren't – like the bars – tended to be places where people sat down and didn't move again for a few hours. Leo looked like he was already a couple of drinks in, sitting with a few friends.

He matched his court photograph well. He was no longer wearing a suit – clad in a loose plaid shirt with the sleeves rolled up, a gray undershirt, and jeans with frayed knees – but he had the same close-cropped beard and short dark hair. He also had a look to his eyes that Tara didn't like, a darkness that went beyond their color.

Tara stopped the car where they were, putting on the parking brake and swiping the keys just for safety. If it hadn't been a populated area, she might have even left the engine running. She didn't see this taking long. He was a prime suspect, and he needed to come to the Sheriff's station with them to get a statement on record – standard practice given the restraining order. She just hoped he was going to volunteer to come instead of making it difficult for everyone.

Glenn got out first, walking around the front of the car as Tara joined him, timing it so they could walk over as a united front. The drinkers saw them coming as they crossed the street, and Daley even downed the last of the amber liquid in his glass as if he fully expected they were there for him.

"Leo Daley?" Tara said, though it was more of a formality at this point than a real question. It was clear that it was him. Not only did he match their photo, but he was also exactly where his current live-in girlfriend had said he would be.

"What's it to you?" he snapped, a tired old response that Tara was sure made him feel like some kind of action hero from TV.

"We'd like to speak to you at the Sheriff's station," Tara said, gesturing behind her to the car. "Would you please come with us, sir?"

"No," he said, and gave a half-laugh as if he couldn't believe they would even ask. "Why do I need to come with you?"

"You're aware of the recent events involving Kimmie Hutson?" Glenn asked, leaving just enough room for the man to make it clear to them whether he really had heard or not.

"She's dead," Daley said, and though there was a flicker of what seemed to be sadness or regret in his face, it was soon gone. "We saw her brother post about it ten minutes or so ago. Everyone was chatting about it. It's got nothing to do with me."

"We need to talk to you as a matter of procedure," Tara said. She was hoping he would hear those words and understand the subtext – the fact that he was obviously always going to be someone on their list due to the history between them, all of which was on record. The fact that he already knew was potentially believable, but for him to have no emotional reaction at all just ten minutes after hearing the news was incredibly suspicious. "I think it would be better to do that in a private setting, don't you?"

*Don't you want to do this somewhere where your friends don't have to find out you're a violent asshole to your girlfriends?*

But Daley snorted, shaking his head at them. His hand was still loosely holding the base of his empty glass, a fact that made tension curl at the base of Tara's spine. If he decided to get up, smash it, and start wielding the jagged edge around… "I'm not going anywhere," he said. "Just because some crazy bitch is dead, I don't need to talk to anyone about it. I told you, it's got nothing to do with me."

There was a general shifting and uneasiness among his friends. Tara was desperately trying to keep a read on the situation. Either they thought he was being an idiot by antagonizing cops and they were wanting to get away from him, or they held views that their friend shouldn't be harassed at a bar by the local pigs. It was hard to tell which way they went. A lot of them were looking down at their own drinks – both the friends he was sitting with and the people at neighboring tables. Was that just a desire not to get involved?

"We need you to come in, Daley," Glenn said. His tone was firm. There was a pair of handcuffs attached to his belt, and he reached for them meaningfully. "One way or another. It would be better for everyone if you just come quietly, say what you have to say, and get it over with."

“Screw you,” Daley said, jumping to his feet. The rickety outdoor chair he’d been sitting on scraped back against the concrete flooring and clattered against the wall of the bar. “I’m not coming with you, one way or any way. You’ll have to try to pin this on someone else!”

“If you’re innocent, the best way to clear your name is to come with us now and answer our questions,” Tara insisted, trying to calm the situation. She had one arm extended out towards him, a kind of safeguard in case he lurched towards her. Thankfully, the glass had remained on the table, and he was almost wobbling on his feet. Too much alcohol in the warm weather, not enough food. A typical Sunday for a lot of these boys, she knew.

Then it happened.

Daley reached down and grabbed the glass after all, almost knocking over one of his friends in the process. The second the glass shattered against the wall, everyone in the vicinity jumped back. The friend who had almost toppled lost his balance a second time, the chair going over onto the ground, and he rolled to get away. It seemed that even Daley’s friends weren’t confident they were safe with him.

Tara drew her gun as quickly as she could before he could approach them, Glenn doing the same. They were a few paces apart, triangulating Daley, both getting him in their crosshairs before he took another step.

“Put the weapon down!” Glenn demanded. “Drop it!”

“Don’t you shoot at me!” Daley screamed, even though they weren’t.

“Drop it!” Tara shouted back at him, hoping their words were somehow going to get through. “Drop the glass, right now! We have you cornered, Daley. There’s no sense in this!”

Daley had a stupid look on his face, like a drunk man wrestling with a question he didn’t understand. He looked like he could go either way.

“Leo, for God’s sakes,” the other friend he had been sitting with exclaimed. “Stop it, or your poor ma’s going to have a heart attack before the day’s out.”

That, at least, seemed to get through to him. He lifted his eyes to Tara and Glenn one last time – moved the glass slightly up in his hand like he was going to use it – both tightened their hands on their guns, aiming them squarely at him –

And he dropped it, letting it shatter into even more pieces on the ground.

The breaking glass could have injured someone in the fall, including himself, but at least he was now without a weapon.

"Hands behind your back," Tara demanded, stepping forward with her gun still pointed at him. When she got close enough, she holstered it, letting Glenn keep his weapon on the man just in case. She spun him around and grabbed his offered wrists, snapping them into a pair of cuffs from her own belt. "You're under arrest for attempted assault with a deadly weapon. Let's get back to the station and get to the bottom of this – before you do anything else you're going to regret."

***

Tara sat down on the chair facing Daley in the interview room, giving him a long and hard stare as Glenn sat behind her. They hadn't been able to give him as much of a cooling-off period as they would normally have liked. He had belligerently refused a lawyer, saying that they were all out to get him, too, but his blood alcohol limit had come back as being within a reasonable range to conduct an interview with him. Maybe he wasn't drunk, after all.

Maybe this was just how he was.

"Leo Daley," Tara began.

"It wasn't me," he said immediately.

She closed her mouth and stared at him.

"I didn't have anything to do with Kim," he said. Give him enough space, Tara thought, and he was going to say enough to incriminate himself with no interference from them. "I wasn't even in town last night. I couldn't have done it."

"Where were you, then?" Glenn asked.

Daley stared at him like he didn't understand the question. "What?"

"If you weren't in town, then where were you?" Glenn repeated. Tara was beginning to see a shift in her perception of Daley as a suspect. He wasn't a smart man – not smart enough to construct a convincing lie that wouldn't fall apart on examination, she thought. He'd specifically said he couldn't have killed Kimmie because he wasn't in town. If he had known that she was killed outside of town – if he had been the one to do it – then, surely, he wouldn't attempt to use that as an alibi?

"I was out with my friends," Daley said.

"Which friends?" Glenn asked with some impatience.

"I don't know. Just some friends," Daley shrugged.

"Daley," Glenn said, sighing sharply. "If you don't tell us their names, we can't use them to check up on your alibi. If we can't check your alibi, we're going to hold you as a suspect for up to forty-eight hours until we get enough evidence to put you away for real. Do you get that?"

"You have to check up on my alibi?" Daley said. He looked troubled.

Tara wanted to roll her eyes. "Of course, we have to check," she told him. "Daley, are you lying about where you were last night?"

Daley looked at the table. He was shifty, moving one of his legs up and down. "No."

"You were out with friends."

"Yeah."

"And you're not going to tell us their names?"

"Well," Daley said, and he shifted again. "Could I get immunity?"

Tara's jaw would have hit the floor if she wasn't trying to keep a professional mask on her face. "Immunity from what?"

"From what we was doing," Daley said.

Tara and Glenn exchanged a look.

"You want immunity for being involved in Kimmie's death?" Glenn asked.

"No!" Daley exploded. "I told you, I didn't have anything to do with that! Just… immunity from something else."

Tara was on the edge of having had enough. "How about this," she said. "You tell us exactly what you're talking about, right now. Because if you don't, we're going to go ahead and find out from someone else anyway, and you're not going to get any immunity. In fact, the judge is going to look down on you pretty hard if you weren't the first one to confess to what you were up to."

Daley swallowed.

"We just heard about one of the cabins being empty for a couple of weeks," he said. "That's all. We just wanted to make a little extra cash."

Tara raised her eyebrow. She was beginning to feel like a high school principal telling off a naughty kid. Or maybe a middle school principal, at that. "What did you do to the cabin?"

"We went inside," Daley said, shrinking into himself a little.

"Through the door?" Glenn asked pointedly.

"Yeah," Daley said. "Well, no. We had to break the window first."

"And you took things?" Tara prompted.

Daley nodded. "I got a TV and some jewelry."

"Are you going to tell us the names of your friends that were there with you?" Tara asked.

Daley nodded, seeming to get smaller and smaller as the moments wore on. He was refusing to look up and meet their glances.

Leo Daley was a dead end. He was a deadbeat, sure – a waste of space and oxygen. A petty criminal who beat his girlfriend and a thief of opportunity. But he was also a coward. Tara didn't know if, ultimately, he could have gone up against Kimmie once he'd been warned to stay away, especially with the threat of Ryan looming over her shoulder. Not only that, but his alibi was another crime – and even he couldn't possibly be so stupid as to confess to one bogus crime in order to try to get himself out of another.

Either way, they could ask one of the junior deputies to check it all out and make the official arrest. Plus with the fact that he'd just threated a Deputy and a Deputy Sheriff with a broken glass, he was going nowhere fast.

But in her gut, Tara knew; it would all check out. Leo Daley wasn't their man.

He had been an excellent suspect – but he wasn't their man.

Which meant they had a drawing board to go back to, and fast, before their leads began to disappear.

# CHAPTER FIVE

He sat back, keeping his sunglasses over his eyes, turning his head in one direction but looking in another. It was easy to pretend to be sitting around doing nothing, living on easy street. It was easy because people saw what they wanted to see and nothing else.

With his head turned towards the windows of the café as if he was watching people go by, but his eyes looking off at a right angle, he could actually watch the man he was here for.

He looked down for real at his coffee, picking it up and taking a sip. The coffee was good, admittedly. The man must have had good taste. It was a shame, really. That taste wasn't going to help him at all in the long run.

No amount of taste could save anyone from having to face him, not once he had them in his sights.

He stretched his fingers a little, bending them against one another, feeling the pull across his palm and the give of his knuckles. It was important to stay in good shape and be ready. He would need his hands soon.

The man he was here for finished his own coffee and got up. The man – Camron - didn't take his empty cup over to the counter to make it easier for the staff to clear it away. Of course not.

He scoffed a little under his breath, finished his drink in one last swallow, took it to the counter, and still made it to the door in time to watch Camron going down the street.

As expected: Camron was walking up towards the center of town.

This was a routine he had observed for long enough now to be confident in it. He had spent a long time observing, in fact. A lot of observation in preparation for a spate of activity, because he knew he had to work fast. If he did not work fast, there was a possibility that the very disruption his actions caused might prevent him from finishing what he had set out to achieve. This was why it had to be today. It had to be now.

Camron turned left, again as expected, making his way up towards his workplace. He knew Camron was going to head in there and pick up his paycheck, then head home. This was always the way. Several weeks of watching, and the pattern never differed on a Sunday.

He waited and watched in the reflection of the glass from a real estate firm, pretending he was looking at properties. A few minutes to go in, say hello, ask for the paycheck, receive it. And… yes, there he was. Camron was leaving his workplace, ready to walk up the hill and head for home.

Everything was going exactly to plan.

He did not wait any longer. He was confident that Camron was proceeding in exactly the way that he was supposed to. That meant he could proceed to the preordained place and wait there, quietly, and still, until it was time.

He walked swiftly – far faster than Camron, who was older and less fit, who had already spent some of his prime years and had consequently slowed down a considerable amount. There was no need to worry about being overtaken. Besides, Camron would stop at the corner store and buy some flowers for his wife.

He took long strides and maintained a constant rhythm, getting himself to the spot where he knew he could prevail. He had already left his car here earlier, ready and waiting. This would be his exit strategy. It had worked last time, after all.

He got into position and waited. Waited. Waited.

Camron stepped into view.

"Sir?" he said, walking forward and holding up a hand.

Camron paused as he looked up. "Um, yes?" he said, taking in the uniform. They always took in the uniform.

"Are you Alec Camron?" he asked.

"Yes," Camron replied, his brow furrowing. He was concerned now.

"Thank God," he said, feigning relief. "I was sent to try to track you down on your way home from work. There's been an accident, and I need you to come with me immediately."

"An accident?" Alarm flared in Camron's face. "What kind of accident?"

"It's your wife, sir," he said. "I'm sorry to have to tell you this, but we need to get to the hospital right away. It was touch and go, and we don't know how long she'll last or if she's going to pull through."

Camron paled. "Oh God," he stammered. "Oh – oh God. I need – I need to…"

"I have my car here, sir," he said. "Please, come with me right away. I'll get you there as fast as possible."

Camron either didn't look too closely at the car or he didn't care. He should have noticed that it was unmarked. Anyone who looked closely and thought logically would ask why it wasn't marked.

The panic over his wife took away Camron's ability to look closely and think logically. This was all by design.

Camron dropped the bouquet of cheap flowers he was holding on the sidewalk, rushing forward to get into the car with him.

"Thank you, Deputy," he said, grabbing the door open. "Please, I need to be with her."

And Camron got inside the car, buckling himself in.

He got inside the driver's side, pressing a button to lock all the doors as he started the engine. "Don't worry, sir," he said. "I'll get you to where you need to go."

## CHAPTER SIX

"I'm not seeing it," Tara sighed. She folded her arms over her chest. "I'm just not seeing it."

"Me neither," Glenn admitted. Tara glanced at him and then sideways at the Sheriff, who was also staring at the board on the wall.

They'd put up everything they knew. The location, full details of the victim, the injuries she had sustained and what they indicated. The mental health difficulties she'd had, the suspect who had been cleared.

"It seems to me we have the perfect suspect," the Sheriff muttered. "Only, it wasn't him."

Tara nodded. "I just don't understand what must have led her up to the mountain," she said. "The only thing that would make sense would be that she was meeting someone there, and yet…"

"Absolutely nothing on her phone, on social media, in her emails, or on her laptop about going to the mountain," Glenn answered for her. "She should have been out in town last night. She was supposed to meet her usual group of friends."

Tara glanced out of the window. It was getting into evening again. It was almost, in fact, twenty-four hours since Kimmie Hutson should have met those friends – except according to all the witness statements they and the other deputies had gathered so far, not a single one of them had seen her.

"There's a piece of the puzzle that we're missing," Tara said. That much was obvious enough. "What about her meds? What was she on, again?"

"Bupropion," Glenn supplied.

"What are the possible side effects of that?" Tara asked.

Glenn pulled out his cell phone and started searching. "Give me a second… here. Uh, headaches, rashes, dizziness, insomnia, anxiety, confusion…"

"Right there," Tara said, pointing at him. "Anxiety and confusion. What about alcohol? Could it have interacted negatively?"

"Let me look," Glenn said, reading aloud as he checked. "Uh… okay… with alcohol… can increase the risk of… hallucinations, delusions, anxiety – yeah, it could have made everything a lot worse."

“So, that could be a reason for her going up the mountain, couldn’t it?” Tara mused. “Maybe she had a drink on her own before meeting her friends. She potentially had a bad interaction with her medication and experienced some kind of delusion or hallucination that pushed her to go up the hiking trail for some reason – maybe she believed she was in danger or that she had to go up there to find something.”

“But a delusion or hallucination couldn’t have killed her,” Glenn pointed out. “That was done with someone’s hands. She couldn’t have strangled herself.”

“Maybe she met someone up there,” Tara suggested. “Someone who was already up the mountain, too. Someone who didn’t want to be disturbed for some reason. She might even have attacked them first if she was delusional.”

Glenn chewed his lip for a moment. “If that happened to me, I might not want to come forward,” he said. “No evidence, no cameras in the area, no way to prove that she really did attack me first. I might think I would end up in prison if I came forward.”

“Which means our job is going to be near impossible,” Tara sighed, dropping her head.

“Not impossible,” Sheriff Braddock spoke up. “Difficult, but not impossible. Easier if the two of you go home, get some rest, and come back at this fresh tomorrow.”

Tara looked up at the board again, shaking her head. “It feels wrong, going to bed,” she said. “Like we’re letting her down.”

“We don’t have any new leads,” Sheriff Braddock pointed out. “I’m going to leave a couple of people on duty overnight just in case anything else comes in. If it does, we can call you back in. But right now, the best thing you can do to advance this investigation is get some sleep – so you’re ready to go when something does come up.”

“Come on, T,” Glenn said, reaching out to pat Tara on the back of her shoulder twice. “Let’s go rest.”

Two against one. Tara rubbed a hand over her face and nodded in resignation. “Alright,” she said. “Under protest, you understand.”

Sheriff Braddock chuckled. “We all understand.”

Tara grabbed her things from her desk and walked towards the exit, managing to coincidentally time it at the same moment as Glenn. They kept pace with one another down the hall and into the parking lot. They had been partners for long enough now – just under six years – that their lives almost seemed to flow in the same direction naturally.

“Don’t stay up all night thinking about it, T,” Glenn said as they parted ways to go to their individual cars. Glenn sometimes drove in and sometimes walked, depending on what else he was planning after work that day. Of course, working in the Sheriff's department, sometimes 'after work' didn't really happen.

"I won't," Tara promised with a sigh. "It's only worth going home if I actually do get some sleep."

Still, though, as she unlocked her car and got behind the wheel, she couldn't shift the feeling that she was letting their victim down by not continuing to push hard during that crucial first twenty-four hours.

And letting victims down led, as it naturally must, to thinking about her sister.

Tara's mind was full of Cassie as she pulled out of the parking lot and turned her car towards home. She hadn't yet fully had time to go over what she had read in the file, to deep dive into every piece of evidence that had been found. It wasn't an official investigation, so it wasn't like she could tell Sheriff Braddock she wasn't to be disturbed. And anyway, this case, Kimmie Hutson's case, was new and current: here, she could actually hope to make a difference.

She wasn't sure she would be able to do the same for Cassie. She knew she wouldn't be satisfied at all until she tried, but she was going to have to fit it in where she could.

Tara pulled up outside her own home and killed the engine, sitting and thinking in the silence for a moment. The only companion to her thoughts was the quiet clinking of the car as it settled. Cassie had been gone for so long. Any physical evidence, of the kind they were looking for in Kimmie's case, would be beyond retrieval. The chance of finding any further clues about what happened to her were so small, it was almost not even worth thinking about.

Almost.

Because if there was even one chance, one shot so small that even numbers couldn't encompass how small it was, Tara would still try for her baby sister.

She grabbed her cell phone off the seat next to her and hesitated, about to open the door and go into her home. One thought seized her as she looked at the phone. There was another person out there who had the drive and the ability, one other person who had access to law enforcement resources but also had enough emotional investment to care about Cassie this much.

Their oldest sister – Jessy.

Sheriff Strong might not be able to help immediately, but she could provide something else. A sounding board. A listening ear and a shoulder for when things became too hard. Tara could at least have someone to talk to about all of this.

But talking to Jessy these days felt like more trouble than it was worth – more of a chore than a relief.

Tara shook her head impatiently and got out of the car, unlocking her front door, and heading inside. It was quiet in her home – it always was. Living alone meant always coming back to a cold, empty place. It was a far cry from the way she had grown up, with two sisters filling the house with noise and arguments, color, and warmth.

But maybe that was what happened after you lost someone so deeply it didn't seem there was any chance of ever getting them back.

So much for getting sleepy, Tara thought glumly, dumping all her things on the coffee table, and switching on the television. An hour of something mindless in front of her eyes and maybe she would drop off. That was going to have to help.

She slumped across the sofa without bothering to change out of her uniform, turning her head towards the flickering images on the screen. She'd found a microwave dinner in the fridge to listlessly spoon through, occasionally managing to convince herself to take a bite of the unappealing stuff. There was protein in it, carbohydrates, fiber – things she needed to keep going tomorrow. That was the only way she could convince herself to get through it.

She sighed and settled back into the cushions once it was gone, laying back with her legs stretched right across to the other arm of the sofa and her head propped up on the one closest to her. The show was not what she would call exciting, but then again, she didn't want it to be. She let it fill her head and push out everything that was keeping her awake – Cassie, the explanation for how Kimmie had ended up halfway up a mountain and dead, who the perpetrator might be, Jessy, Cassie again.

She didn't even notice her own eyelids closing until she was fast asleep, the television continuing to quietly play away to itself into the early hours.

## CHAPTER SEVEN

"Sit there," the stranger had said, and Alec Camron kept his mouth shut and did as he was told. He didn't really have a choice.

Mentally, he was testing his boundaries. He was bound hand and foot, not able to get up on his own – he'd tried flexing his leg muscles a little to test it, but he was confident now that he couldn't stand and run away. Even if he did, he would only be able to hop.

That was the mistake he had made. He could identify it now. He should never have allowed the stranger to tie him up.

"My wife," he said faintly, hearing his own voice disperse to the wind outside the entrance of the cave. The stranger had made him kneel there, his hands and bound ankles both behind him, looking out across the incredible view of the state park and the town beyond. "She's not really in danger, is she?"

"I told you," the stranger said. "If you came up the mountain with me, she wouldn't be harmed. I made you that promise."

It was all becoming so confusing in his head. First, Michelle had been in some kind of accident. He'd believed that even after the Deputy had turned off the road onto the mountain trail. He'd believed it right up until he switched off the engine and looked at him, and told him that his wife was fine – but she wasn't going to be for long if Alec didn't comply.

Now, he wasn't sure whether he understood if Michelle was actually alright or not.

The way the stranger – the Deputy – had phrased it, it sounded like he wasn't working alone. Maybe he had someone out there right now with a gun at Michelle's head. Maybe he was watching her through the windows of her home, watching how she paced backwards and forwards while she waited for her husband to come back. He was late – very late. She had to be worried.

"Are you going to let me go back to her?" Alec asked, hearing how his own voice wavered, how the wind took and stole it. The cold air was making him shiver. He'd dressed for the warmth of the day, but now, up here, the night was freezing.

"No," the stranger said, and Alec closed his eyes for a moment.

He didn't know what was going to happen to him. He didn't want to ask. He didn't want to get the details. He'd heard a story in town when he went for his paycheck – a story that was circulating around all the locals about a young woman who had been found in the caves. They were saying she had been bound and tortured to death, or that she had been strangled, left for a couple of terrified boys to find. Lydia Peablossom, one of the town's big characters who seemed to know everyone and everything, was holding court in the café, telling everyone about how one of the boys was in shock and still hadn't spoken a word since it all happened. When he went to get his paycheck, one of his coworkers had said in hushed tones that someone was doing ritual murders up there.

He hadn't even listened to any of it, but now he was running back those conversations in his head and they made him shake all the harder. He was in it, now. He was bound in a cave in the night, and he knew what had to be coming next.

He needed to get away from here before that happened.

"Something much better than going home is waiting for you," the stranger said behind him. Alec couldn't see him from here. He didn't dare turn his head. He kept looking out at the view, the beautiful view. The town was lit by tiny specks of light, an orange glow hanging over it all. Even in the darkness, his eyes had adjusted to pick out the shapes of rocks littered across the relatively light-toned trail, the spikes of trees around them. From right here, there was a gap through the trees that looked all the way down to the other side of Wyatt and beyond. He could work out, if he concentrated on the patterns of the lights, exactly where his home was. Exactly where Michelle was waiting for him.

*Oh, God,* Alec prayed silently. *Give me a way home. Please. Show me the way to get out of this.*

"What we are talking about is enlightenment," the stranger said. He had been talking the whole while, but Alec couldn't concentrate on him for more than a few moments at a time. "That is so much bigger than this life. Enlightenment is a worthy goal for anyone. Enlightenment is redemption."

Alec couldn't move his hands far enough to get at the ropes, or even to reach anything on his ankle that would help to get his feet free. He felt like he was kneeling in front of a firing squad who insisted on giving him a lecture first. Was the lecture really for him? What was he supposed to do with this knowledge if he was never going home from this cave?

"You must ascend the planes," the stranger was saying, and Alec thought he sounded unhinged, like he didn't even have any connection with reality anymore. "That's what you have to understand. That's what all of this is about. You brought it on yourself, but it's all over now. I'm here to help you."

*Oh, God, help me*, Alec prayed. *God, please, show me a way to escape. Show me how I can run away. Can I trip him? Can I talk him out of this? Can I make him repeat this lecture over and over again all night until the sun rises, like Scheherazade? Will the light of the sun make this whole nightmare dissolve and show me that it was only a dream? Show me a way to –*

Alec barely even felt the blow that came from behind, the sharpness of it, the heaviness of the impact on his head. He only knew that he was praying one moment, and in the next moment, he knew nothing at all – his eyes open and seeing nothing, his head finally empty of any thoughts, his soul – if he had one – no longer trapped on the mountain.

## CHAPTER EIGHT

Tara was staring into the waters of the lake when she heard it.

She had been here so many times, looking for Cassie. At first with purpose, and then without. She had been here for so long, she probably knew this place better than her own bedroom. She could look around easily and see that *these* small stones near the shore had moved since her last visit, that *this* piece of driftwood must have been deposited by the water sometime in the last week.

She was looking at the driftwood when the voice called out, and Tara knew immediately who it was that was calling her.

"Cassie!" Tara called back desperately, leaping to her feet, the word tearing out of her throat like something important that she was never going to get back again. She listened hard, and –

"Tara!" Cassie called back. "Tara, help me!"

Her voice was distant, like she was far away or underground or even under the water. Tara spun in a circle, looking all around. She couldn't see a single sign of anything, nothing that would tell her where her sister was.

"Cassie?" she called out again. "Cassie, keep talking! I can't see you!"

"Tara," Cassie called back, and Tara couldn't figure out what direction it was coming from. Left or right? Up or down? Where was she supposed to be looking? The wind was whipping up around her, seeming to toss Cassie's voice in every direction as she called out.

"Just hang on," Tara yelled. She fell to her knees on the rocky shore, pushed by the wind, kneeling on the uneven ground, and hanging on for dear life. "I'm coming, Cass – just hang on!"

"Tara – Tara, help me!" Cassie screamed, her voice becoming more shrill, more desperate. "Tara, help me!" Her words descended into a scream, a scream of pain and fear that went straight down Tara's spine and sent her frantic, left her turning and turning in every direction for some sign. The scream became higher and then more rhythmic, more like a pattern or a tune, and –

Tara opened her eyes to the sound of her phone ringing and sat bolt upright on the sofa, for a moment completely disorientated. She was in her living room. The TV was still on, an early morning rerun of a nature documentary, a howling storm of wind on the screen. She grabbed the remote and jabbed it off, reaching for her phone and putting it to her ear before checking the screen.

"Hello?" she said, clearing her throat to rid it of the telltale sound that she had been asleep until a moment ago.

"Deputy Sheriff, it's Bryant," the young Deputy said. "I'm just about to leave the station, but we've had another body reported."

"What?" Tara rubbed at her eyes desperately, trying to wake herself up fully. It was dark in the room without the TV on. "What time is it?"

"Just before five," Deputy Bryant reported. "It's in another cave up in the mountains."

"Wha – hold on," Tara said. There were a million questions going around and around in her head. "Text me the coordinates when you're on the way there yourself. I'll call Glenn and get him up."

"Yes, ma'am," Deputy Bryant said smartly, hanging up the phone on his end.

Tara groaned out loud as she scrolled through her contacts list. Her back and shoulder were stiff from lying on the sofa all night instead of getting into her bed. She found Glenn's name and hit call, prying herself up from the sofa to stumble towards the stairs. She needed to change into a fresh uniform, maybe try to grab a three-minute shower if she could get the time.

Glenn answered after five or six rings. "Tara?" he asked, his voice just as bleary with sleep as hers had been.

"Need you to come pick me up," Tara said, not bothering to try to formulate anymore full sentences until she'd at least gotten changed. "Been another body."

Glenn made a groaning noise that might have been a slurred curse in response. "'Kay," he said. "Be there in ten."

There were a lot of questions beginning to gather in Tara's mind as she ran under the shower and out again and then dressed. Who was up in the mountains before dawn? What had they found, and did the body match the MO of Kimmie Hutson's killer? Who was the newest victim? Would it be someone that Tara knew? Was the body a fresh kill, or had it been waiting in the caves for a while without being discovered?

Did they have another killer on their hands, or was this the same perpetrator as before?

And if it was the same – was he going to stop at two?

A buzz on her phone screen called Tara's attention as she tried to hurriedly dry her blonde hair, and she looked down to see a text from

Glenn telling her he was outside. She cursed, dropping the hairdryer, and switching it off at the wall, and then scrambled to her feet. She was still shoving her feet into her boots as she stumbled outside and locked her front door, then piled into Glenn's passenger seat.

"Good morning," Glenn said, without any trace of irony, as he set the car going along the road. Tara leaned down to tie her boot laces, bracing herself as the car turned sharply to the left and she found herself almost thrown into Glenn's side.

"Are you kidding?" Tara muttered darkly. She finished her first boot and moved onto the second, hoping they weren't going to be involved in a car crash before she was done. She didn't rate her chances in a head-on collision when her face was pretty much in the dashboard.

"It's always a good morning when I get to work with you," Glenn chuckled.

Tara stared at him. A faint blush came over his cheeks as he glanced over at her.

"What? Too cheesy for this time of the morning?" he asked. "I can't believe it. Tara Strong, not being in a good mood first thing?"

Tara scowled and swatted at him, not really intending to hit him at all, her hand only swishing through the air. "Watch yourself, or I'll show you how good of a mood I'm in."

Glenn burst out laughing, but it was only a few seconds before he sobered up. The mood in the air was too grave for real levity. "What have you heard about the body?" he asked.

"All I know is it's in the mountains," Tara said. She sighed. "When Bryant called me and woke me up, I wasn't in the right frame of mind to be asking those questions. But it's suspicious in the timing, right?"

"It has to be the same killer," Glenn said confidently. "It's a double murder case. Who else is going around out there killing people hiking up mountains?"

"Their own cardiovascular systems, mostly," Tara muttered. There was still a chance. Still a chance this was just a coincidence and not another complication. Not another murder on their watch.

But it was such a slim chance that she didn't even believe it herself as they drove over.

***

Tara paused to wipe her brow, looking down at the trail they had come from. Somewhere down there, too far now to be seen, they'd had to leave Glenn's car. Like before, they had parked right next to the patrol car – Deputy Bryant's. He must have had to abandon it when he found the trail narrowing and steepening. The Sheriff hadn't yet arrived, which meant Tara knew she was going to be the most senior officer at the scene.

The way was tough even though the sun wasn't yet fully up. Dawn was breaking over the town below, a sight which should have been reason to stop and watch and maybe take pictures. They didn't have time for that, this morning.

"How much further to go?" Glenn asked, panting for breath as he paused, too. He put his flashlight back in his belt; they had needed it for the first leg of the hike, but now that the sun was rising, things were easier.

"I'm not sure," Tara said. She had the coordinates from Bryant, of course, but the way ahead was so steep they were going to have to climb at certain points – like the climb she'd just had to make, scrambling up a few instances of rock walls that were almost as tall as she was. Her arms were aching already, unused to this particular type of exercise. "From the map, it's not too far. In terms of height, though, it's another matter."

"Great," Glenn said. He grabbed the bottle of water he was wearing hooked into his belt loop and took a sip, glancing around. "It's really steep. I don't know how anyone would get up here."

"They'd have to be far too strong to climb this while carrying a body," Tara said. "The only way I could even think it could be done would be by tying the body onto your back like a backpack. Even then, the sheer weight of it would be incredibly difficult to carry. On the areas where you have to climb, I would even suggest it would be impossible."

"So, how does he get the bodies up there?" Glenn asked.

"Yes," Tara nodded. "That's the question." She gestured up ahead, a throw of her hand that meant *let's keep going*, and started to walk again.

The cave loomed into sight after they had scaled the next series of three drops, each one requiring a little more energy than the last. Tara leaned on her knees and panted for breath as she looked at the view one last time before turning to Bryant. He was waiting for them near the entrance of another cave, just like he had been at the last crime scene.

There was a man sitting on a rock beside him dressed in what looked like camping gear: warm, waterproof clothes, thick socks visible above sturdy camping boots, a woolen hat guarding him against the cold night air. She assumed he had to be the man who found the body.

If he was a suspect, he probably wouldn't be sitting there so soberly and calmly.

"I didn't go inside much," Bryant said, approaching them with a pale face. "I thought I'd better wait for you or the Sheriff."

Tara did not like how pale his face was, or what it might imply about what was waiting for them in the cave.

"You did good, Bryant," Tara nodded. "Stay with our witness. Glenn and I will take a look."

She turned to plunge headfirst into darkness once more, hoping that this cave would not be as cramped and oppressive as the last – and that it would reveal the secrets of the killer that they desperately needed to catch him.

# CHAPTER NINE

The body was easy to find. Tara almost tripped over it on the way in. It was right by the entrance, as if the killer had no regard for really, properly hiding it. As if he just wanted to dump it somewhere out of the elements and leave.

She knew enough to understand that what she saw in the beam of her flashlight was a fresh body, not an old one. There were no signs of putrefaction to be seen, and when she cautiously touched the arm with a gloved hand, it felt stiff and cold. So not an old body, but not a brand new one – it had been there for more than a few hours but less than a day. She would feel better when Lindsie verified that for her, but for now, it was a loose guideline to work with.

"Watch where you're stepping," Tara told Glenn, though it was probably unnecessary – he knew what he was doing.

They had to be careful about disrupting any evidence before they'd had a chance to examine it properly. Tara dropped to her haunches and shone her light directly at the ground around herself, checking for any sign that might be useful. Both the cave itself and the ground outside were dry, so there were no footprints or other marks they might be able to use. Tara had little hope they would find anything useful; if this crime scene was like the last one, he had been careful.

"There's a tunnel leading back," Glenn said. He was standing still but twisting to look around, clearly not wanting to risk another step. His flashlight was picking out a jagged rip through the rock at the far side of the cave. "Well, kind of a tunnel. I can't see how far back it goes. It's pretty thin."

Tara nodded. "It probably leads nowhere, like in the last cave. These kinds of places have pockets like that everywhere. It's just where the water once flowed to carve out the space, but it doesn't mean we'll be able to get through."

Glenn smirked at her – she saw his expression in the light she shone past his face. "You just don't want to admit that you're claustrophobic. You'd say anything to get out of exploring that tunnel."

Tara rolled her eyes. "If that was it, I'd just send you," she pointed out. "We can't go any further until we can set up a proper light, anyway. Let's get the Sheriff, Lindsie, and a couple more deputies up here to help out. The victim can't tell us much right now, anyway."

Glenn nodded. "I'll make the calls," he volunteered, stepping backwards through the entrance of the cave as if to keep to his own footsteps.

Tara looked down at the victim one last time before turning. A man, this time, not a woman. Their victim profile could not be gender-based; there had to be something else linking him to Kimmie Hutson. Maybe he was an ex, or a potential new suitor. He looked older, and a wedding band flashed in the light on his finger, but that might not mean anything.

Still – an older man would be much heavier than a young woman. She was more convinced than ever that there was no way anyone could climb up here carrying the body to hide him. And Kimmie had been killed in the cave, anyway; they knew that from the blood evidence on the stone floor.

Both of these victims must have climbed or hiked up to the caves on their own.

But why?

It was perplexing for Kimmie Hutson to do it – and even stranger, now, for someone to climb up after hearing that a young woman had been murdered in one of the caves at night.

Which had her wondering about the man who had found the body.

She stepped outside, noticing Glenn a few paces away on the phone, and nodded at Deputy Bryant. "This is the man who found the body?" she asked, looking more at the man for confirmation than at Bryant.

"Yes," he said, stepping forward. "My name's Peter. I'm camping down at the foot of the mountain, in the campground there."

She thought she remembered a turnoff for a camping site just before they had to pull up and stop. Tara turned and looked down. From the very edge of the ridge, she thought she could see maybe the top of a tall campsite entrance sign. She stepped back towards the witness, satisfied she understood where he was talking about.

"Peter," Tara repeated, looking him up and down to get the measure of him. He seemed the outdoorsy type, although also a little timid in the face of law enforcement. Nothing she saw about him indicated any signs of a struggle or suggested that he was an immediate suspect, but she kept an open mind. "Can you tell me what you were doing up here so early in the morning?"

"Oh, I wasn't," Peter said. He made a rough gesture with his hands, his words tumbling on like he was nervous. "What I mean is, I wasn't up here to begin with. I only came up here to find the body."

Tara narrowed her eyes at him. "How did you know there would be a body?" she asked.

"Oh, uh, no," Peter said. He gave a half-laugh, then a glance back towards the cave that turned the corners of his mouth back down. "No, sorry, I'm a little flustered. I've never seen – well, you know…"

Tara nodded. "I understand," she said, more to get him to move on than anything else. "So, why did you come up here?"

"I saw a flashlight," Peter said. He mimed turning around and gesturing to the sky. "It was up here, someone flashing a light around in what looked like all directions. I thought they might be lost. I climbed up this trail yesterday, so I knew the way and how to get down, and I thought I should go and see if I could help them. It's too far to shout, so I just set off."

Tara watched him closely, wondering if she bought his Good Samaritan story. "What did they say when you caught up with them?"

"Oh, I never caught them," Peter said, shaking his head solemnly. "By the time I got up here, they must have found another way down. I cast about a bit and saw the cave. I thought they might have given up and gone in there for shelter – it was cold last night. I shouted hello but no one answered. I looked in with my flashlight just in case, and that's when I saw him."

"Did you call the police immediately?" Tara asked.

"No, I couldn't get cell service up here," he said. Tara checked her phone and saw that he was right. She glanced around and realized that the reason she couldn't hear Glenn talking anymore wasn't because he was quiet or because she had mentally blocked him out – he must have gone down a way to get a signal himself. "I hiked back to the campsite first and then called. Then I waited over here at the foot of the trail so I could lead this Deputy who came first right up to the cave."

"I called you before I came up," Bryant supplied, having listened to the whole thing. "He pre-warned me about the signal."

"Okay," Tara nodded, looking back over the edge of the ridge. You could see a lot from up here. The campsite was down below to the left, through the trees. Straight ahead you could look over Wyatt. To the right, more mountains rose, cradling the national park, camping grounds, and the lake systems that took up a good chunk of Edgar County. "What did he look like, this stranger?"

“I didn’t see that either,” Peter shook his head. “The flashlight was bright enough and the night dark enough – I couldn’t see anything at all. I don’t even know if it was a man.”

Tara looked at him sharply. Was that supposed to be some kind of clue? But, no – he was just shrugging his shoulders, guessing. She was being a little too paranoid, maybe. It just seemed like these difficult and obscure trails were suddenly getting more traffic than she’d ever noticed in a life of living in Wyatt.

But then, there were thousands of trails out here. Thousands of paths up the mountains, thousands down. The lakes and the forests had their own trails and routes. It was both part of the challenge of working in Edgar County and its charm. The people were few, those who were around were often tourists, but it was an example of how stunning nature could be in a very visceral sense.

“You didn’t pass him on the way up? You’re sure?” Tara asked. “Where did his light go?”

Peter shrugged again. “I’m sorry,” he said. “I was looking down, concentrating on my feet. I didn’t want to trip and end up falling all the way back to my tent. I guess he must have gone past me somehow – there’s probably more trails around here, maybe down one of the other faces of the mountain from here, or maybe he went higher up to go down at another point and go around me.”

Tara nodded, mostly to herself this time. She was thinking. There was no sign of any tracks on the ground, nothing that might indicate to them where the killer had gone. There was no point in bringing in someone who could read tracks, either – there wouldn’t be any, not unless he had disappeared into the trees, and even then it would be incredibly hard to trace him.

No, Peter was probably right. The killer had seen or heard someone coming towards him and simply made good his escape in another direction. That was easy enough to work out, much harder to prove. Once again, they were looking at a dead body which had almost no answers for them – and a hell of a lot of questions.

Glenn was coming back up the trail. Tara turned to Bryant; with three of them now on the scene, they could afford to shuffle some things around a bit. “Why don’t you take Peter back to his campsite?” she suggested. It wasn’t far, and either Bryant would be back or the Sheriff and the other deputies would arrive, allowing Tara and Glenn to move onto other tactics. “We need to start thinking about how to get an ID.”

"Oh, I have his ID," Bryant said. He fished in a pocket and pulled out a notebook. "He had a wallet with him. I checked it – there's cash inside and no empty spaces for cards, so I don't think anything was taken. And I read his driver's license."

Tara read the name he had written out in block capitals. "Alec Camron," she read aloud. "Alright. Good work, Bryant. And his address, too."

Bryant beamed at the praise. He ripped the page out of his book and handed it to Tara before tucking the notebook away. "Alright," he nodded to Peter. "Let's get you back safe to your campsite."

"The Sheriff won't be long," Glenn said quietly, while Peter and Bryant disappeared over the edge of the ridge and began their descent. "He said he trusts you to have checked everything out, and that so long as there's someone watching the cave, we can head out for interviews. He'll stay here with Lindsie when she arrives."

Tara nodded. It was exactly as she had expected. "We can go speak to Alec Camron's family first," she said. "He was wearing a wedding ring, so bets are good that he lives with someone else."

"Do you think he's connected to Kimmie Hutson?" Glenn asked. His face voiced the concern she'd already come up with. "Older man, younger woman?"

"If both of the victims were connected to their killer in some way, it would explain a lot about why they both hiked and climbed up the mountain to get here with him," Tara said thoughtfully. "That's the only way they'd get up here – willingly, under their own steam."

Glenn turned and looked back down the mountain trail. "Even if he doesn't carry them, the killer has to be fit."

Tara started to argue, thinking that it was possible to get up here even if you weren't completely fit and healthy, but then thought better of it. "You're right. Once he got up here, he had to stay in control of the situation – enough to be able to kill them. He couldn't be out of breath, waiting to get his stamina back. If he left that variable open, he would risk them being able to leave and get away."

"Plus, he must know the trails well enough," Glenn added. "Even if you only came up here once to get the lay of the land, you would want to know how busy it was up here. How many people could see you."

Tara glanced down in the direction of the campsite, thinking. "Or did he mess up? He was seen, just not clearly enough to be identified."

"Was that deliberate?" Glenn asked back. "Did he want the body to be found? Both of them have been. Or was it bad luck?"

Tara turned the other way, looking up at the mountain. She knew from the experience of having lived here for so long that the mountains were riddled with caves. Many of them were nothing more than shallow overhangs or places small enough for an animal to make its home, but others were much vaster. "Or have we only found two out of many more?"

It was a chilling thought. Both stood in silence for a moment, contemplating the mountain.

"We don't have that many open missing persons cases," Glenn pointed out. "None from Wyatt townsfolk."

That, at least, was comforting.

But Tara couldn't help wondering.

What if they had a lot more on their hands than they realized? Could it be that their murderer was on a larger killing spree, and they just hadn't seen it?

## CHAPTER TEN

The family home that Tara parked outside was foreboding. Not because it looked badly kept or had any red flags that put her on edge: quite the opposite. It looked like a lovely place to live.

Which meant that it was probably home to a family who cared for it and each other – and she was about to break the news to them that the man of the house was dead.

Tara took the lead, anyway, walking out ahead of Glenn towards the door and knocking firmly on it. It was still early morning, though the sun was fully up. She wasn't even sure if anyone was going to answer the door.

When it was opened, within a matter of mere seconds, she was taken aback.

A blonde woman with a robe clutched around her body was there, clearly wearing modest pajamas underneath. There were dark circles under her eyes. When she saw Glenn and Tara, her first expression was one of disappointment – but as she took in their khaki uniforms, it quickly cycled to fear and alarm.

"What's happened?" she asked. "Where's Alec?"

Tara swallowed. It took all her willpower not to glance at Glenn for support. It wasn't Tara who needed it – it was Mrs. Camron. "Can we come inside?" she asked.

The woman went pale and stepped back inside the house, allowing them to follow her. She walked straight through to a living space that was bathed in early-morning light, sitting down on a plush white sofa with a numb expression on her face.

"I'm sorry to have to tell you this," Tara said. She couldn't find any way to soften her words enough to make it easier to hear. She never could. "But we found a body this morning. We have reason to believe it's that of Alec Camron."

Mrs. Camron was already pale and shaking, but with those words she seemed to crumple in on herself. She sank deeper into the cushions of the sofa, her face breaking, her hands slipping over her eyes as she began to sob.

There were an awkward few minutes as Glenn and Tara stood in this unfamiliar, spotless room, surrounded by framed photographs and knickknacks that spoke of a life lived together. Mrs. Camron cried, and they waited. There was nothing else they could do.

Eventually, Glenn had enough; he looked at Tara and made a helpless motion with his arms which she interpreted as meaning, *isn't there something we can do*? Tara bit her lip and then moved over to sit beside the grieving woman on the sofa, slipping an arm around her shoulders. Mrs. Camron sagged gratefully against her and continued to cry, shaking up and down against Tara's arm.

"How?" Mrs. Camron finally asked, when the storm of sobbing seemed to have subsided enough for her to manage to get a word out.

"We're still investigating," Tara said. "At this moment, it's very early stages. However, we do have reason to believe that he may have been a victim of foul play."

"Someone…" Mrs. Camron gasped for breath. "Someone killed him?"

"It looks that way," Tara said. "I know this is a very difficult moment for you, but the quicker we can find some answers for our investigation, the more likely it is that we'll be able to figure out what happened to your husband. Can you answer a few questions for me?"

Mrs. Camron sat up on her own, taking a deep shuddering breath and wiping her hands over her eyes. Tara watched her carefully. She had seen this kind of reaction before. The woman was mostly likely in shock. That could make this dangerous – anything could set her off again and make her fall deeper into her grief, making it impossible to get any more answers out of her for hours or even days. They needed to get these questions answered now before it was too late.

"Yes," Mrs. Camron said, nodding. "I'll tell you whatever I can."

"Alright," Tara said. She kept her voice low and gentle, not wanting to startle the poor woman. Any moment, she might realize the reality that hadn't yet fully set in – that her husband was not coming back home ever again. "Did Alec tell you anything about going to the mountain yesterday? Perhaps going hiking or climbing?"

"No," Mrs. Camron said. She looked down at her hands. "I've been waiting for him to come home all night. Worrying. He never came home yesterday after he went into town to pick up his paycheck. He always comes home and brings me flowers on Sundays." She made a loose gesture into the corner of the room; Tara saw an empty vase sitting in prime position on top of a dresser, ready and waiting.

Tara bit her lip for a second, thinking how best to proceed. "Did he mention meeting anyone? Has he ever met anyone after work or on the way home?"

"Not without planning it in advance," Mrs. Camron said. "If anything ever delayed him, he would let me know. He would call me and make sure it was alright."

Tara nodded. "Has his behavior at all changed in the last few months?" There could be signs that might explain this. Secretiveness, if he was having an affair. He might have become jumpy or worried if someone was threatening or blackmailing him.

"Not at all," Mrs. Camron said with a slow shake of her head, crushing that line of thought entirely.

"Can you think of any reason why he might go up the mountain?" Tara asked, grasping at straws but needing to check.

"No," Mrs. Camron said. She raised her hands a little in the air and then dropped them again. "I just don't understand. Is that where he was?"

Tara paused sympathetically. "I'm afraid so," she said. "Is there anyone around him, even in his past, that you think might wish to cause him harm? Or anyone he had argued with?"

"No, I can't think of anyone," Mrs. Camron insisted. "He's a normal man. We have a normal life. Why would this happen?"

"I can't answer that yet," Tara said sadly. Her heart was breaking for the poor woman. She was obviously unable to fully comprehend yet what was happening – not an easy task when you didn't even have all the details. "Do you know someone named Kimmie Hutson?"

Mrs. Camron shook her head again, but her eyes widened. "Oh, God," she said. "I heard her name on the news last night. She was killed too, wasn't she? Was it the same person?"

"I don't know yet," Tara told her honestly. "You're sure you never heard the name before last night?"

Mrs. Camron shook her head, her eyes drifting down as she fell into thought.

Tara was running out of things to ask that would get them anywhere. She glanced around. Glenn made a sharp gesture at her with his head; from how pointed his eyes seemed to be, Tara got the impression he'd been trying to get her attention for a short while. He jerked his chin to the side; he was standing by a bookcase, and Tara scanned her eyes over it.

There was a photograph there of a man in climbing gear. The same man who was pictured in the wedding photographs on the wall. The same man, in fact, whose face Tara had looked into that morning in a cave.

"Mrs. Camron," Tara said. "Did your husband climb?"

The woman looked at her in confusion, then followed her gaze to the photograph. "Oh," she said. "I'd forgotten about that. Alec wanted to get into it. My brother bought him a voucher for his birthday last year for some lessons with an instructor. He went along and did all the lessons that had been paid for, but as soon as the voucher ran out he just stopped. He said he wasn't that interested in the hobby after all."

"Do you remember the instructor's name?" Tara asked, because it might be something. It could be nothing, but it was related to the mountain, and that was a good enough reason to look into it.

"No," Mrs. Camron said. She squinted over at the photograph, as if remembering. "The gear was all rented. I think it has the name of the instructor printed on it."

Glenn picked up the photograph in its frame, bringing it closer to his eyes. "Yeah, it's printed on the edge of the harness," he said, turning it sideways to read. "Looks like… Dorian something? Dorian Bell?"

"Dorian Ball," Mrs. Camron said suddenly. "I remember now. We laughed about it because…" She trailed off, leaving the reason unspoken but obvious enough. Her eyes glazed over slightly. Tara knew what that looked meant. She was reliving a memory – and realizing at the same time that there would be no more.

"Mrs. Camron, is there anyone who can come over and stay with you?" Tara asked. "A family member, a close friend…?"

"Yes," Mrs. Camron said distantly. "Yes, I'll call my brother."

"Do that now," Tara instructed her. She didn't want to leave the woman alone for too long. "And if something comes to mind over the next few days, no matter how small, please mention it to us. We'll be able to take your call any time of night or day." She took a card out of her pocket that had her personal line information – direct to the phone at her desk in the station, which, if no one answered, would divert to her cell phone.

She watched as Mrs. Camron picked up her own cell, dialing her brother's number. As soon as the call connected and she needed to speak, she burst into tears; Tara figured that would get the message across more than anything else.

Tara walked into the hall to give Mrs. Camron respectful privacy, Glenn following behind her. "I'll stay until her brother gets here," she told him. It wasn't a good idea to leave a family member alone like this; you never knew what their reaction might end up being if they were left with their thoughts. Things could get dark. “We need to look into this climbing instructor – Dorian Ball.”

“I’m on it,” Glenn nodded smartly. “What about the car?”

“I’ll let you know when I have some indication of how long it will take him to get here,” Tara said. “If you’re busy by then, I’ll get someone else to pick me up. Or I’ll just walk back to the station – it’s only fifteen minutes from here if I keep up a good pace.”

“Got it,” Glenn said. For a moment he looked awkward, like he didn’t know how to leave – how to say goodbye. Tara had a feeling that he was going to try to hug her, which would have been inappropriate given the context. Then he looked back at the door to the other room, as if to convey his sympathy towards Mrs. Camron, and he stepped out of the front door.

Tara walked back in just in time to hear her say something about seeing her brother soon and she ended the call. She put on her best customer-service face and gave Mrs. Camron a brave, encouraging smile. “Shall I make you a cup of coffee?” she asked.

As annoying as the delay was, this was procedure. She would have to rely on Glenn to tackle the next part of the investigation – and she was glad she could count on her partner to have it handled.

# CHAPTER ELEVEN

Glenn sat in his car outside the Camrons' home, scrolling through things on his phone. He found the number he had saved for the Hutsons – a matter of course in any case, because you could need information from the families at any given time – and hit dial.

He glanced up at the house again as the rings beeped in his ear. To lose your life partner – it was a horrible prospect. He couldn't imagine going through it. Then again, it wasn't like he was in a relationship. Not like that, anyway. He was still relegated to having unrequited feelings from afar –

"Hello?"

Glenn recognized the voice as Ryan Hutson, their first victim's brother. He must have been the first one to get to the phone. "Ryan, hello," he said. "It's Deputy Grayson. I have a quick question if you don't mind?"

"Go ahead," Ryan said. "It's about Kimmie?"

"Yes, it is," Glenn told him. "Do you know if she ever went climbing on the mountain?"

"Uh…" Ryan paused. Glenn could almost hear him thinking. "Yeah, she did once. We both did. Hold on. Mom?"

Glenn held the phone away from his ear for a moment as Ryan yelled back and forth with his mother. The woman's voice was too far away to make out exactly what she was saying.

"Yeah," Ryan said. "Yeah, she went for some lessons with some of her friends out of high school. They picked it up the summer after they all graduated, but then the others all went to college and Kimmie stayed here. I took one of her friend's unused vouchers and did a few lessons with her, but then she ended up not doing it anymore. Dorian Ball – that was the instructor she was with."

"Dorian Ball?" Glenn repeated. "Are you sure?"

"It was a few years ago, but yeah. Mom just reminded me. I remember we kind of laughed at his name."

Thank goodness for juvenile humor, Glenn thought. "Alright, thank you," he said.

"Wait," Ryan called out. "What's this in connection with? Is that the guy who killed her?"

"We don't know yet," Glenn said. "He's not even a suspect at this stage. I'm just trying to make connections."

"Connections between what? Has there… has there been someone else?"

Glenn closed his eyes for a second, cursing himself. He'd let it slip, hadn't he? "We found another body on the mountain this morning, in a different spot," he said. "I'm afraid that's all I can say at this moment in time."

In fact, it was more than he should have said. Ryan tried to ask another question, but Glenn cut him off with a hurried goodbye and hung up the phone. He looked at the screen in thought. It wasn't much of a connection between the two victims. They wouldn't even have been taking lessons at the same time. But it was a connection. And it connected them with the mountain, too, no less.

He looked up the address for the instructor's business and put it into his GPS, setting off quickly. The sun was shining strongly now, glinting off the cars parked along the residential street and heating up the temperature. It was going to be another nice day.

A shame that they were going to have to spend it chasing after a murderer, making other people's days not very nice at all.

Glenn's thoughts drifted back to Tara as he drove, as if part of him was still back there at the house. He hated splitting up from her like this. Ever since they'd gone their separate ways while investigating the killer who had stalked their lakes recently, and she'd been attacked while Glenn was elsewhere, he hated the thought of her being on her own. Granted, a grieving wife was not exactly the most likely candidate for an attack, but still…

The thought lingered.

Glenn tried to put it out of his head, to call it paranoia. By the time he was pulling up outside a small store with what was obviously a tiny office above it, he had given up.

Worrying about Tara was quickly becoming his life's work, and he wasn't sure he was going to be able to change that no matter how much he wanted to.

Glenn parked and got out of the car, jogging over to the side door that was printed with 'DORIAN BALL CLIMBING INSTRUCTOR' across the glass and pressing the bell beside it. There was a short wait and then a buzz, and he walked through the door and up a set of rickety stairs.

Alone in the stairwell, with no one watching, Glenn discreetly checked his gun. It was there, accessible, loaded. Just in case.

He stepped through another door at the top and into a small but brightly lit white office space with two desks. Looking around to orient himself, Glenn saw no one who might match the description of Dorian – only a young woman behind one of the desks who beamed at him welcomingly.

"Hi!" she said. "Are you interested in climbing lessons?"

"Uh," Glenn said. Most of the time when a Deputy walked in somewhere, the people assumed he was there on official business, not to become a customer of theirs. "Actually, I was looking for Dorian Ball."

"Oh, he's out with a client right now," the woman said smoothly. "Can I book you in for a session with him?"

Glenn gave her a wry smile. "There's no need for the hard sell," he said. "I've already got a bit of climbing experience, anyway. I need to speak to him on a police matter."

"Oh," she said, her voice faltering. Then her expression brightened. "Oh, is this about that girl that was found in the caves? Do you need an expert to consult on the case?"

"Something like that," Glenn said. There was no point in correcting her. Besides, if she knew he wanted to question Dorian to see if he was a suspect, she might clam up. "Can you tell me where he is right now?"

She consulted something on her computer screen. "Let's see… yes, he's on one of our most popular trails. Do you want to wait here for him?"

Glenn shook his head. "Tell me where he is. I'll go there. This is too important to wait."

She looked a little put out at the idea that he was going to barge in on a client session, but Glenn didn't care. For all he knew, this latest client might be Dorian's next victim.

Which was an incredibly worrying thought.

His cell phone buzzed and he checked it to see a message from Tara: *Brother is five minutes away*. Perfect timing.

They had a mountain to climb, and Glenn was relieved that they would at least be able to do it together.

***

Glenn looked up at the mountain face ahead of them. It was the same mountain where the two victims had been found, but that hardly meant anything at all. There were so many faces to this thing, rising from the earth, and all of them had different attributes.

While the trail where Kimmie Hutson was found was reasonably easy to walk, and the trail where they had discovered Alec Camron required only a small amount of climbing that could be done without a harness, the area where Dorian Ball had taken today's client was a series of sheer faces broken with plateaus between them. There was no walking up here.

You had to climb.

"Is this right?" Tara asked him, tugging at one of the buckles on her harness. Glenn looked around to see what she was doing and nodded.

"Yeah, that looks safe," he said. He reached out and gave one of the side straps a tug, making sure it wouldn't budge. "You should be good to start climbing."

He wasn't sure how he felt about this. Dorian Ball's assistant had assured them that they would only need the harnesses to climb – they kept a number of semi-permanent ropes and handholds on the rock face, since Dorian led lessons there almost every day. She'd even said that they wouldn't face any difficult climbing up alone so long as they clipped their harnesses into the rope system. With his climbing experience, Glenn knew how to do that.

But there was still the nagging thought that they were using a system set up by a killer – one who might be willing to cut said ropes in order to take care of a couple of deputies trying to stop him from escaping.

"Let's go, then," Tara said, walking to the first set of ropes. Glenn swallowed hard. She was really going to do this, wasn't she? Sometimes he thought Tara was fearless – and that scared him more than anything. It meant there was a chance she might do something stupid in the name of getting justice.

"Are you sure you want to do this?" Glenn asked. "We could just wait for him to come down."

"First, he might not come down," Tara said, looking up as Glenn clipped her into the system. "We don't know if he might see us down here and make a run for it. Or he might be up there attacking his victim right now, which means we have a duty of care to get up there and try to save a life."

"And second?" Glenn asked glumly, clipping his own ropes.

Tara launched herself towards the rock face, grabbing onto the first handholds and lifting herself up until she could fit her feet on top of the lowest ones. "Second, I have actually done this before, so stop worrying about me," she said with a laugh.

Glenn swallowed hard again, looking at the holds in front of him. She was already climbing. There was nothing to do.

If she was going to throw herself right into danger, then he was damn sure he was going to be throwing himself right alongside her.

They began to climb silently. They had no way of knowing how far up the mountain Dorian had managed to go. If he was training someone completely new to climbing, there was a chance it could take him a long time to get up each face. With that in mind, Glenn and Tara could catch up to him – or catch him on the way down, if he was going faster.

Glenn watched Tara as much as he watched his own ascent. It wasn't a difficult climb, in particular. The handholds were spaced well, meaning you could easily reach each one without stretching. There was no need to carry a pick with you and jam it into the rock with each movement, using it to haul yourself upwards. If you needed a break, you could lean back and let the rope take you, knowing it wouldn't let you drop down unless you reached up to release the catch. The distance wasn't so far, and between each climb there was a place to take a break.

Glenn found himself climbing onto the first plateau ahead of Tara, unhooking himself from the ropes and then moving back to the edge. He knelt on the stone, ready to reach down and offer her a hand to help her up.

"Stop waiting," Tara said, waving a hand at him as she paused.

Glenn stayed where he was, stubbornly, reaching down until she took his hand. "We might as well help each other," he said, then pulled hard, taking half her weight as she hauled herself up the short distance to the edge.

"No," Tara told him. She was a little more breathless than he was. "You're clearly faster than me. You should keep going. If there's someone in danger up there, every minute could make a difference. Just go until you get to the top. Be careful and watch out – if he's waiting up there to strike, we might not even see him until we're over the edge."

Glenn nodded with gritted teeth. He didn't want to go ahead on his own. He wanted to stay back and watch Tara. What if she fell? What if she didn't hook her ropes up properly and the catch didn't hold, and she ended up plummeting back towards the ground?

It didn't even cross his mind until she said it to worry that he himself might be in danger, but that was hardly anything.

And what if he got attacked right at the top, leaving Tara unaware, following him into the same trap with no chance of backup?

"Go on," Tara said, already unhooking herself and walking over to the next set of ropes. "That's an order from your superior officer, you know."

Glenn sighed. She was pulling the Deputy Sheriff card. He moved to his next rope and surreptitiously watched her hook herself up, making sure she did it correctly. Only when he was satisfied that she was safe did he begin his own climb. "Fine," he said. "But if you need me, you call out. Don't stay quiet because you want me to get the jump on Dorian Ball. It's too dangerous up here."

"Yes, sir," Tara said ironically, and Glenn reluctantly focused on his own climb.

He was no stranger to moving up the rock face like this. He'd climbed many of the natural mountain surfaces around Edgar County, and spent a good bit of time learning at indoor climbing walls. If he really needed to, he could probably make this climb without the ropes and harness – although he had no intention of taking that risk. He focused on hauling himself up one hand, one foot, at a time, until he reached the next plateau and climbed up onto the steady ground.

There was no one here. Glenn looked upward, aiming his gaze at the top of the next climb. From the ground, they had been able to see that this was the last section with ropes. After this, the mountain was steeper and more difficult to climb, making it a good natural endpoint for lessons.

Which meant that, more than likely, Dorian Ball was right at the top.

Glenn practiced reaching for his gun. The harness was difficult to get around, impeding his movements. If it came to it, he wouldn't be able to draw fast enough to beat someone else with a gun. But from what they had seen so far, their killer used his own strength, not a firearm.

So Glenn could hope, anyway.

He looked around as he started the first few handholds to see Tara coming up over the edge behind him. Unlike Glenn, she didn't waste any time hanging around or resting – she headed straight for the next set of ropes, closing the distance between them. Good. Glenn didn't want to leave her too far behind, no matter what she had said.

He made it almost to the top of the climb, one hand steadily over the other, and then paused.

Over the edge of this cliff, Dorian Ball was either killing someone, waiting for him to get close enough so he could strike, or completely unaware that a Deputy was closing in on him.

Glenn took a deep breath and pulled himself up, popping his head up over the edge just enough to look around.

There was a man across the far side of the plateau, which was such a large, open space it was more like a mini summit. A perfect landing stage, a site where someone could easily camp for the night before continuing their climb if they wanted to.

The man turned slightly and Glenn recognized him from the posters in the office. Dorian Ball. It was him.

And he was… alone?

Glenn looked left to right but saw no one else. Dorian had stood up from where he was seated on the far edge, and now started walking towards him. Glenn hastily pulled himself up the rest of the distance and scrambled to his feet, not wanting to be caught unaware by a killer.

Where was his client? Where was the person he was supposed to be up here with? Had he killed them already?

"Dorian Ball," Glenn shouted, his voice carried by the breeze across the open space. Dorian nodded, hearing him easily. Behind him, Glenn was aware of the sounds of Tara pulling herself up the last part of the climb.

Glenn's heart caught in his throat. Dorian didn't seem worried at all. Glenn's eyes were caught by the narrow opening of a cave at the other side of the plateau, almost invisible except as a shadow down the rock face.

Were they so late already that he was confident they weren't going to find the body?

# CHAPTER TWELVE

Tara hauled herself up and over the edge of the rock, looking up to take stock of the situation as quickly as possible. Glenn was in front of her in a ready stance, his hand looking like it wanted to stray towards his gun.

Across the flat space, the man that she figured must be Dorian Ball was approaching casually, lifting a hand in greeting.

"What's up?" Ball called out. "Were you looking for me?"

Glenn stayed tense, his hand hovering in the air over his holster. Tara scrambled to her feet, wrestling herself as free of the harness as she could be without actually taking it off. Glenn needed her backup.

"Where's your client?" Glenn asked. His voice was sharp and tight, the tension crackling. Tara's heart pounded as she conducted a visual search of their location. There wasn't a single trace of another person – not even another harness.

"Oh, is that who you're after?" Dorian asked. He came to a stop a hundred or so feet away. He was beginning to react to the tension in the air, to what must have been Glenn's sharp expression, to the fact that he was facing two armed members of the Sheriff's department who did not seem happy. "He never showed up."

There was a pause. Tara wasn't even quite sure she understood what she had heard. "Are you telling us that your customer didn't arrive for their session this morning?"

"Yeah," Dorian said, looking between her and Glenn as if trying to understand what was happening. "Has he done something wrong? He didn't call to cancel or anything. I waited down there for half an hour, but he just never showed."

"Why are you up here if you don't have a client?" Glenn asked, a question that cut right through Dorian's chatter with the urgency and insistency of his tone. It was the million-dollar question, Tara supposed. How could he justify that?

"This is one of my favorite climbs, so I thought I'd just come up here anyway and get the practice," Dorian shrugged. "It's nice to get the fresh air and stay fit. Sorry, has something happened?"

Glenn looked at Tara, waiting for her guidance. Tara looked back at Dorian. Could she believe him?

There was nothing disingenuous about his movements or his voice. He looked genuinely surprised to see them, and now genuinely worried that he didn't understand what was going on.

Tara sagged.

He was telling the truth, wasn't he?

"Call back down to the office," Tara told Glenn quietly. "Do you have signal up here?"

Glenn pulled his cell phone out of his pocket and checked it. "Yeah."

"Get the number of the client and call him," Tara said. "We need to verify that he's still alive."

Glenn nodded quickly. He put the phone to his ear, though his eyes followed her as she took a few steps closer to Dorian. She felt it. He was as wary as she was, knowing that they could easily be listening to the words of a killer who knew he could tell them a lie and they might not have any choice but to believe it.

"Do you know Kimmie Hutson?" Tara called over to Dorian, taking another couple of steps closer.

"Uh," Dorian said, thinking. He was stepping closer to her as well, though cautiously. "Yeah, I think so, maybe? I think I taught her a few lessons ages ago. It sounds familiar. Can't tell you the details without checking my records, though."

"And Alec Camron?"

"Oh, I definitely know him. He was in one of my classes last year. He had a voucher. He did the whole course and then I just didn't see him again after that. I don't know if he carried on climbing on his own or not."

Behind her, Tara could hear Glenn talking to the office. She pressed on. "Have you heard anything about those two names in the media recently?"

Dorian's brow furrowed. "No, I don't think so," he said. "Has something happened?"

That question again. It might be innocent, or it might be for show. Maybe he knew full well what happened to them. "I'm afraid that both of them are dead," Tara said. She gave no extra details. She didn't even mention that they were both in caves. She didn't want to give him anything that they could use to identify the killer. If he let something slip about the caves, then she would know she had him.

Dorian's face fell at her words. "Oh," he said. "Oh, no. Oh, that's so terrible. What happened to them? Was it a car crash, or something?"

"No, it wasn't a car crash, Mr. Ball," Tara replied. Behind her, Glenn had gone silent; he must have been making the second call. "They were murdered."

"Both of them?" Dorian's eyes widened, his mouth dropping open. "But… that's… that kind of thing doesn't happen around here!"

Clearly, he hadn't heard about the killer targeting women by the lake they had recently caught – either that, or it was all part of a convenient act. But paranoia was starting to wear thin on Tara's mind. Could she really suspect everyone? Dorian was acting innocent enough. He really did seem shocked, even devastated, by the news.

"Hello, is that Mr. Smith?" Glenn was asking behind her. "It is? Okay, great. And you booked a climbing lesson for this morning? You slept in? Fantastic, thank you. That's all we needed."

Tara glanced at him, then back at Dorian. He was telling the truth. His client this morning was still alive.

Did that mean he wasn't their killer?

"Where were you last night or early this morning?" Tara asked.

"At home, asleep," Dorian answered immediately. That was the problem with nighttime murders. Always so hard to alibi.

"Can anyone verify that?" Tara asked.

Dorian seemed to think. "I guess, my girlfriend?" he suggested. "She was asleep too, though. We were both pretty tired out from Saturday night."

Saturday night – that piqued Tara's attention. "What were you doing Saturday night?"

"It was our annual Scouts night," Dorian said. A grin lit up his face. "We come out to the mountain with a group of boys and teach them how to climb. We take them up the easiest face on the mountain – it's around the other side. There's a big shelf, about three times the size of this one, where an old peak fell off thousands of years ago or something. We set up camp, tell ghost stories, and then stay there all night. The three of us that lead the camp take it in turns to watch over them all night in case someone gets out of their tent in the dark and creeps toward the edge."

A solid alibi, then. Tara nodded. She could finally accept that Dorian was who he said he was. Of course, they could double-check and make sure that no one had seen him sneak off in the middle of the night, but it was highly unlikely that he would be able to get back around the mountain – since the site where Kimmie was found was closer to where they stood now – go up the trail, kill her, and head back, all without being spotted.

But now that she was sure he was innocent, there was something else that came to Tara's mind. Dorian was a climber, and he obviously knew the mountain reasonably well. Maybe there was a chance he knew something that could help them.

"Can you help us out with a few questions?" she asked. She stepped closer to him easily and freely now, knowing he wasn't their killer. She could lower her voice, with no need to shout across the distance. "We could do with an expert's view on a few things."

"Wow, yeah, of course," Dorian said. He shrugged, relaxing more in response to her and putting his hands in his pockets. "What do you need help with?"

"Our victims have both been found in caves on this mountain," Tara said, and Dorian's eyebrows rose high.

"What? Wow. Okay, now I understand why you wanted to see me," he said. "Jeez. Okay. Shallow caves or deep ones?"

Tara glanced back at Glenn uncertainly. How did you measure a cave? Was it height or length? "I don't know," she said, given that Glenn didn't appear to have an answer either. "They were small antechambers, I suppose."

Dorian nodded. "Okay. Any signs of animal activity?"

Tara shook her head.

Dorian nodded again and looked around himself, as if he was searching his memory for the kinds of caves that might have been used. "There are a lot of those on easy trails," he said. "The human activity – people using the trails regularly – tends to keep the animal activity down. If it was higher up, you'd probably have a mountain lion or at least some birds having a go at the body within a few hours."

"Do you have a map of the trails?" Tara asked, inspiration seizing her.

Dorian reacted quickly, nodding, and reaching back to take off the backpack he was wearing. He slung it down onto the floor in front of himself and grabbed a folded piece of paper from one of the pockets. It turned out to be a map of a kind, though not the type that Tara expected. It depicted a thin section of brown and green land, with blue lines seeming to wriggle all over it.

"The first one was on the East Eagle trail," Tara said, giving its official name. Dorian quickly pinpointed a blue line and followed his finger up it until he hit a marking which, she assumed, indicated a cave.

"Right here," he said. "What about the second one?"

"Uh," Tara hesitated, realizing she hadn't taken the name.

"The Bandit trail," Glenn put in.

"The Bandit trail? Really?" Tara asked.

Dorian chuckled. "They said that bandits used to wait in the caves to ambush people who were passing by," he said. "Of course, that was before the landfall that made that area a lot steeper, like it is today. Alright, I know where you're talking about."

"Would it be possible, in your opinion, to carry a dead body up to those caves?" Tara asked. This was what had been weighing on her, what she really needed to know. If she was right in her suspicion, then it was a big clue about the MO of their killer.

"No," Dorian said decisively. "For Kimmie, maybe. I don't know what size she would be now, but women tend to be lighter than men. But Alec – I remember him. He wasn't overweight, but he was heavy enough. I don't think anyone could make that climb while carrying him. Even if you found a way to strap him to your back, it would be too much. You'd have to use equipment. Did you find any marks or holes in the rock face?"

"No," Glenn spoke up. "I spoke with the Sheriff on the way to pick you up, Tara. He said there wasn't any evidence of climbing equipment after they'd done a more thorough examination of the scene."

"Then they must have been alive when they went up there," Tara said triumphantly.

It was a big clue. To have it confirmed felt like it must be something of a breakthrough. The killer had some way, some method of convincing them to get to the top of the trail and go into the cave before he killed them.

The most obvious answer would be that it was someone who was known to them.

A shame that ruling out Dorian had brought them this clue when it seemed to be one more piece of the puzzle that would have made him an excellent suspect.

"Thank you," Tara said. "You've been a huge help."

"Anytime," Dorian said. He seemed struck by an idea. "Hey, would you want me to start checking out the other caves? I can climb to most of them pretty easily – there's just a few near the peak and some on the east face that are really hard to get to."

"No," Tara shook her head. "We don't want to put any civilians in unnecessary danger. There may not be any other bodies – and you could end up putting yourself right into his line of fire if you come across him bringing another of his victims up. I don't want to be knocking on your girlfriend's door in the morning to tell her that we've found your body."

Dorian paled a little at the image. "Okay," he nodded in agreement. "Well, the offer's there if you do need to check anything out."

"There is something you could help with right now, if you don't mind," Glenn said.

"What's that?" Dorian asked. Tara also watched him curiously.

"Well, we've got to get back down to carry on our investigation," Glenn said sheepishly, gesturing to the cliff edge and their patrol car so far below.

# CHAPTER THIRTEEN

Tara hadn't even managed to finish opening the doors to the station before she heard a familiar voice calling out her name.

"Strong – Grayson! Get over here!" Sheriff Braddock bellowed, and for a horrible second Tara thought they must have been doing something wrong.

Then she managed to get a clear view of the room and saw that the Sheriff was standing in front of a briefing board – a whiteboard with a map stuck on it and the pictures of their victims, as well as some salient details about their crime scenes. The rest of the deputies were gathered around him.

"Sir," Tara said, quickly moving to join her colleagues.

"You're just in time," Braddock continued. "I'm about to give a briefing. Last time I spoke with Glenn, you were on your way up the mountain, or I would have called you back in."

"We just got done," Tara said. She looked down for a moment, wishing she had better news to deliver. "It was a dead end."

"Alright," Braddock said, gesturing to a couple of chairs – the ones in front had, conveniently enough, been left empty. Tara snuck over to them with Glenn close behind her, feeling like she was the last one getting into class. "Where was I?"

"You were telling us about our next steps," Collins spoke up officiously.

"Right," Braddock nodded. He gestured towards the map on the board, which looked strangely similar to the one that Dorian had just shown them. "We don't know if there are any other victims. We're not sure whether the killer got unlucky these two times, or if he intended for us to find the bodies. If it was bad luck, then we could be looking at more victims – and if there are more victims, there may be more evidence. One theory I've been ruminating on is that the killer lives up there in the mountains. It could explain a lot. If the victims went up there for some other reason – some reason we don't yet know about, such as maybe a secret meeting with someone who might not wish to come forward – then maybe they stumbled into his territory. I think that we need to check this mountain out. If there's a living place up there in the caves somewhere, or if there are more bodies, we need to find them."

"How are we going to know where to look?" Deputy Bryant spoke up. Tara frowned. She wasn't sure that she believed in this theory of someone living on the mountain. There had to be a reason why Kimmie and Alec had gone up there in the first place, and an affair didn't ring true – nor did it explain why they had gone up there on different nights.

Sheriff Braddock made a dour face. "We don't, unfortunately," he said. "Which is why we're going to need to organize one of the biggest search operations we've ever unfolded in this county. We're going to have to search every cave on that damn mountain – all that we can access, anyway."

There was a general murmuring among the deputies – Tara heard someone behind her muttering about how long it was going to take. Her heart sank. "Sir," she said. "I think I've made a mistake."

Sheriff Braddock turned towards her with his brows beetling down over his eyes. "Strong?"

Tara took a breath. "I was just speaking with a civilian," she said. "He's a climbing instructor. He offered to help search the caves as he's familiar with them. I turned him down because I thought it was too dangerous for a civilian to get involved, and too big an undertaking. Should I give him a call and tell him he's needed after all?"

Sheriff Braddock nodded slowly. "You made the right call," he said. "It would be far too dangerous for a civilian to go alone. But he can help us out with the mapping and coordination, and he might join a team for searches."

Tara nodded. She made to get up. "I'll go and call now," she said.

"Hold on," Sheriff Braddock said, holding up his hand. "I'm not finished yet. Now, I know you're all thinking that this is too big a thing to do, just like Deputy Sheriff Strong said. We're going to divide things up between us so we all know we've completed the right caves. Some of us that can climb will take the more difficult trails, and those of us who can't climb will take the walking trails."

"This is still huge," Glenn said, going a little pink at the ears when all eyes turned towards him. "There must be hundreds of caves on that map. There's only ten of us. Even if we manage to check out several caves a day with all hands on deck, this could take a long time – and we won't be able to give any attention to other crimes that might happen while all this is taking place."

"You're absolutely right," Sheriff Braddock said unexpectedly. "We don't have enough manpower, pure and simple. Which is why I'm not proposing we do this without help."

Help?

Like drafting in locals, as Tara had stupidly refused with Dorian Ball?

"Did someone call the cavalry?"

The sound of that familiar voice in this familiar place was jarring, too much of a mismatch. Two things that did not go together.

Tara swung around in her seat and stared incredulously as her sister, Jessy Strong, led a dozen deputies from her own county into the room.

"Ah, Sheriff Strong," Sheriff Braddock said. "You're right on cue. I was just explaining to the team here how we're going to split the caves between us."

"That's right," Jessy nodded. Her gaze passed over Tara and through her as if they had no relationship at all, glossing over her and continuing back to the Sheriff. "Never let it be said that Canto Rodado County lets down its neighbors. I'm here, as are those of my deputies with climbing experience, for the duration of the search until you no longer need us."

A dozen deputies. It was probably not even half of the force Jessy had working under her over there in Canto Rodado. It was one of the many things that she enjoyed rubbing in Tara's face at every given opportunity – the fact that even if Tara did one day make it to Sheriff, she was still going to be presiding over the smaller county of the two.

But Tara could put that aside and focus on the good – on the fact that Jessy had come to help when they needed it. She could at least think about that.

"Let's start handing out assignments," Sheriff Braddock said. He paused and looked at Jessy again. "Unless you'd like me to do a case briefing before we start?"

Jessy shook her head with a smile, her glossy blonde hair swishing behind her in a ponytail. "I've already taken care of that with the materials you sent over," she said. "Unless there have been any new developments since the body this morning?"

Tara clenched her fists, out of sight beside her chair. She was the one who was supposed to come up with new developments. She was the one who had failed so far.

"No, there's nothing new," Braddock said, deepening Tara's gloom. "So, assignments. You're all adults. I'll leave it to you to figure out who to partner up with. Go out in pairs at minimum – threes or fours for the harder climbs. Don't try to do anything outside of or above your capabilities. Take bottled water and make sure to stay hydrated – and most importantly, when it gets dark, we pull back. No sense getting ourselves into trouble in his domain."

"We'll stick together, right?" Glenn murmured quickly in Tara's ear as everyone began to stir. She turned and nodded at him. Why would he even think that she would pair up with someone else?

"Tara?"

Oh.

Tara turned to see her sister, making sure to plaster a smile on her face. "Jessy," she said, getting up from her chair. The sisters didn't embrace. At some point they had grown out of that. Maybe grown too far apart. "It's good of you to come down here and help."

"I'm not stealing your thunder, am I?" Jessy smiled.

"No," Tara said, feeling only bitterness towards herself and the fact she hadn't been able to do a better job so far. "No, we need all the help we can get."

"That's what Sheriff Braddock told me," Jessy said, managing to simultaneously make it sound like she was so honored to be asked – and that such a provincial Sheriff had no hope of solving this alone, anyway. "Gosh, your station really is so small, isn't it? Is there more of it around the corner, or is this it?"

"There's just the Sheriff's office," Tara muttered. She looked up at Glenn, who was glaring daggers at her sister. He looked like he was about to get himself into trouble. Tara took a deep breath. "Are you paired up with someone yet?"

"Oh, I'll probably get together with someone from my team," Jessy told her. Tara got the impression that the word 'team' held a competitive meaning in Jessy's head. "We should start organizing. Why don't you give out the assignments for your side? We can take the north and east faces of the mountain, you can take the rest. I'll talk with you later!"

"Now I see why you don't like going home for family dinners," Glenn muttered under his breath as Jessy walked away.

Tara sighed. She turned to him and gave him a lopsided smile, shrugging one shoulder. "She wasn't always like that," she said.

"You don't have to apologize for her just because she's your sister," Glenn said.

"I'm not," Tara said. "Really. I know we get protective here because this is our home, but she's kind of right."

Glenn's eyebrows shot up. "About what?"

"About this being a small station," Tara said. She glanced around with a chuckle. "It's one of the things I like about it, actually. Jessy comes off too strong sometimes, but she's right. She has a bigger county, a lot more deputies, a lot more power. She deals with bigger cases than we do – cases like this – on a regular basis. She left Edgar County because she wanted to do something bigger. I'm glad she's here."

"Really?" Glenn asked. He looked at Jessy's back, over where she was briefing her group quietly. It was like he was reassessing her based on what Tara had said. "You don't feel mad about the way she spoke to you?"

Tara chuckled. "We used to wrestle when we were kids. I'm just glad she got over that phase and only does it with words now. I can handle a few words from the hotshot Sheriff of the next county over, especially when she's earned them." She paused, and looked back at the map. "Besides – she gave us the easy sides of the mountain."

Glenn looked at the map with her, clearly noting the number of caves on each side as well as how difficult the trails were marked as being. "Huh. She made a mistake there!"

"No, she didn't," Tara said. She smiled at her sister's back for a moment, knowing that Jessy had made the offer in such a blasé way to avoid making a big deal out of it. "She grew up in Wyatt just like I did. She knows these mountains better than I do. She and her friends used to go climbing up there on weekends. She knows she's taking the harder part of the task."

"Huh." Glenn cocked his head to the side.

"Anyway," Tara said. She clapped her hands, instantly drawing the attention of the other deputies. She felt Sheriff Braddock's attention on her, too, as she gave them assignments, knowing he would speak up if he thought she was making a bad choice. "Collins and Kay, you take the first batch of caves here following this trail. Stump and Walker, you take the second trail. When you come back down the mountain you should be able to link up with the third trail, here. The fourth trail for Alonzo and Wallach. The farthest two trails on the south side, Bryant and Sheriff Braddock, if that's okay with you both?"

There were nods all around. "What about you and Grayson?" Sheriff Braddock asked.

Tara hesitated. Maybe she shouldn't keep the best job for herself – but then again, someone had to do it, and she was the second most senior investigative officer they had. "We'll do some further work on the evidence we have so far and liaise with our civilian climber," she said. "Try and get a narrowed down window sooner rather than later for where he might turn up next."

Sheriff Braddock nodded approvingly. "Alright, you heard the woman," he said, effectively dispersing the deputies with a word.

"When you finish your trail, radio back to base here and Tracy will send you on your next trail," Tara called out. "And don't forget to pick up your copies of the maps!"

The others rushed out of the room; Jessy and her group had already set out. That left just Tara and Glenn, with the Sheriff lingering behind.

"Good work, Tara," he told her. "We'll make a chief out of you, yet."

Then he was gone, too, and Tara checked her watch. It was midday. Enough time to tell Tracy how to assign each of the new trails when the deputies called back in, and then get on the way themselves.

Maybe, with everyone working together, they could actually find their killer – or some hard evidence to work with, at least – before the end of the day.

"I'll go and give Dorian Ball a call," Glenn said, touching her on the shoulder. "I take it you're going to talk to Tracy."

Tara nodded. "Thanks," she said. "Ask him to meet us here."

She walked out to the entrance where Tracy sat behind her desk, getting a view of the parking lot through the doors as she did so. Jessy was still there, talking to one of her deputies beside their cars, obviously answering some last-minute questions. Tara hesitated, pausing, watching her.

She could go out there and grab her before she left. Tell her she wanted to talk to her about Cassie. About how she was thinking of reopening the case, even though she knew it would reopen old wounds. How she wanted so desperately to find out at last what had happened to their baby sister.

Did Jessy even still think about Cassie? Did her disappearance still haunt her the way it did Tara, or had she simply decided Cassie had to be dead and drawn a line under it? Tara had this feeling like Cassie was going to turn out to be her white whale, the case she could never solve, and it terrified her. Maybe if she spoke to Jessy, her older sister would tell her not to pursue it. Not to try.

But if she brought it up, there was a chance that Jessy *wouldn't* tell her that. And despite all the doubts, Tara knew one thing.

She was going to reopen that case. She had to. Otherwise, Cassie was going to haunt her until the day she died.

What was the point of becoming a Deputy Sheriff if she wasn't going to use the position to do what she had always gotten into this for – solving the mystery of Cassie's disappearance?

She bit her lip. Jessy turned away from the conversation and back towards her car. Her gaze flicked over the Sheriff's station and she raised a hand to Tara. Tara raised one back, waving quickly. Jessy got into the car and was gone.

She'd missed the chance.

"Did you want something?" Tracy asked, and Tara realized she'd been standing there like an idiot for far longer than she had meant to.

"Oh, yes," she said, and put the map down in front of her. "Right, I need you to give out some assignments…"

They could talk about Cassie when this case was done. When they weren't all focused on something else – on what Tara should be focusing on.

Finding the man who had already killed two people in their mountains, before he managed to kill a third.

# CHAPTER FOURTEEN

Tara rushed to hold the door of the station open, beckoning Dorian Ball to hurry inside. He nodded and smiled when he saw her, breaking out into a light jog to get to the door and come inside.

"Hi," he said breezily. "I'm so glad you called. I'm really happy to help, however I can."

Tara was already leading him down the short corridor towards the main part of the office and her desk. "Thanks for coming in," she said, turning over her shoulder to talk to him. She was more than eager to get started. The wait for him to arrive had been interminable. Even a minute's delay rubbed on her nerves at this point. "We have some maps and photographs for you to look at."

"Of course," Dorian said, coming into the room behind her as she rushed him over to her desk, where Glenn was already waiting. "What do you need me to find, exactly?"

"Any similarities or differences between the caves that we might be able to use," Tara said. She was trying to be smart about this. The others were all working hard to comb every inch of the mountains, looking in every single cave. She didn't want to work hard – she wanted to work smart. "We have two victims. What we want is to use this information to identify the most likely places where the killer would take a third."

Dorian looked at her and Glenn with raised eyebrows. "You think this guy has killed someone else?"

Glenn shook his head quickly. "We don't have any evidence to suggest that just now. It's more about being prepared. We also have some reason to suspect he could even be living on the mountain. If so, finding his cave would be really beneficial in catching him."

"Got it," Dorian nodded. He looked down at Tara's desk, which was scattered with crime scene photographs and maps. He swallowed. "So, what am I looking at?"

"Sorry about the nature of the images," Tara said, mindful that he probably would never have seen anything like this before. She'd tried to be as selective as possible, choosing the crime scene photos that highlighted the features of the cave itself, cutting out those which were simply graphic images of the bodies. It wasn't easy to do, and there was a certain amount of inevitable inclusion, but it was nowhere close to the level they had to look at. Still, for a civilian, it was a lot. "These over here are from the first murder, and these from the second. On the maps and landscape photographs, I've highlighted each of the caves."

"Okay," Dorian said slowly, starting to look more closely. He began to sift through the images, picking them up and looking through them. "So, the first thing is that they are on the same mountain, and I guess that's why you already think he might be based there. It's good news because there are even more caves across the other mountains in the range. But this mountain being the last one in the range, so to speak, means it's quite possible he's limiting himself to this location. He doesn't have as many opportunities to cross passes higher up and switch to another peak."

Tara nodded – this was what they had already considered. "Do you think that there's a possibility he might cross to the rest of the range later?"

Dorian shrugged, meeting her eyes. "I'm a climbing instructor, so I'll leave the criminal profiling to you guys. But the benefit, so to speak, of this peak is that it doesn't have such a direct connection to the neighboring mountain. It's isolated with a strip of flatter land between it and the next peak. That makes it a separate climb from one to the other. So, yeah, if he's familiar with this peak and likes it, I guess it's likely he'll stay there."

"Great," Tara nodded. In the absence of an actually trained criminal profiler like the FBI might have, this knowledge about the mountain was golden, as far as she was concerned. "What about the particular caves he's chosen?"

"Well, I do see some very clear defining characteristics for both of them," Dorian said. "In each case you have a large antechamber, big enough for several people to move around in easily, with an entrance that allows you to look out across the surrounding countryside and the towns below."

Tara hadn't noticed that. She grabbed a couple of the photographs out of the pile, images that captured at least some of the view from the cave entrance where Collins had been looking for evidence of entry. "He can see us down below. You think that's significant? Maybe why he chose these sites on these faces of the mountain?"

"Again, I don't really know how killers think, but it does strike me as standing out," Dorian said. "If I was thinking about camping on the mountain in a cave, these would be great choices because you have room to live, a great view, and shelter from the elements without feeling totally cut off from the world."

"Interesting," Tara nodded.

"And the climbs are getting steadily more difficult," Dorian said. "I mean, we only have two examples, but it does progress. The first one is easy to get to. The second one, you have to climb, but you could do it without equipment easily."

Glenn nodded and tapped one of the maps. "I've been wondering whether he maybe chose this one for his first kill because it meant less things that could go wrong. If you only have to walk to the cave, not climb, you won't struggle as much."

Tara made a noise of agreement. "If these truly are his first and second kills, then that progression makes sense. He's gaining confidence."

Dorian's faced blanched a little further. "You think there could be more kills, earlier than this?"

Tara had to remember who she was talking to. "Well, the evidence as we're looking at it now doesn't bear that out," she told him, trying to be reassuring.

He cleared his throat. "Uh. So, like I was saying, the climbs get steeper. So, maybe the next cave you want to find will be an even more challenging climb?"

Tara nodded. "These are good thoughts. He should be on a face of the mountain that looks out over the town, with a large enough space in the cave itself to have room to move, and a more advanced climb than the second site. Are there any caves that would come to mind for you that fit that description?"

Dorian seemed to think for a minute, picking up a map of the caves on the face of the mountain and studying it. "There's a couple. One here, and one here." He tapped each one with a finger as he went, bringing them to Tara and Glenn's attention.

"Two options," Tara said with a nod. "What are the climbs like?"

"The first one is more complex than the climb you had this morning to find me," he said. "There are no rope systems in place on that part of the mountain, the altitude is higher than the previous caves, and neither of these are set up as specific climbing routes. That means there isn't a lot of footfall up there specifically. In fact, I don't even know how often people would have visited that first option. Once a year might even be too high of an estimate."

"And the second?" Tara asked.

"Well, it's more of a popular route," Dorian said. "It's on the main climb to the peak, but off to the side by a few meters. It's not specifically part of the route but I could imagine people seeing it and veering off to explore. I've been up there myself a few months back."

The cave that was off the beaten path, where someone would have to really know the mountain to find it; or the cave that was easier to find and learn about, but subsequently perhaps less private.

How were they supposed to narrow that down?

"The first two caves," Tara said. "Are they on any kind of popular routes?"

"This first hiking trail is only really popular with locals," Dorian said. "It's a good spot for a casual hike and gives a good view of the town, but it doesn't really go anywhere."

Tara thought back to the kids who had discovered the body – just out for a hike to get them out of the house and keep them out of trouble. "And the second one?"

"Much less popular," Dorian said. "There's a camping ground below it, but most people who camp there go for either the walking trails or the climb up where you met me this morning. If they're already serious about climbing, they'll go for the steeper trails to the east."

That was where Jessy was already checking with her team. Tara considered this information, looking over at Glenn. He also seemed to be turning thoughts over in his mind.

"He must live locally," Glenn said. "Maybe he learned all this from living on the mountain itself like we thought, or maybe he used to live in town. He definitely knows where he's going on the mountain. He knows ways to get up and get down in different directions – like how he left the scene before the camper found the second body up there."

Tara nodded. "So following that logic, he's more likely to go for the cave that's less visited. Right?"

"It makes sense," Glenn shrugged.

Dorian nodded himself. "I'll say it again, I'm not an expert in this kind of stuff. But I do know about the mountain. If for some weird reason I wanted to live up there, I would go for a cave that was off the beaten track so I wouldn't get visitors coming and rummaging through my home. And I would never think about bringing someone up here to commit a crime unless it was the kind of climb I could do in my sleep. If he lives up there in that cave, after that difficult climb, then walking up the trails would seem like child's play."

"Then it has to be there," Tara said with a nod. "We have to go there. If we're going to be smart about this and find him fast, then we go to that cave."

"Is it on anyone's assigned route?" Glenn asked, glancing at the larger map they had set up in the briefing area.

"No," Tara said, glancing at it but knowing the answer by heart anyway. "It's on the second list of runs. No one will get to it for hours, if not tomorrow."

"Then we'll go now," Glenn nodded decisively, making the choice that she already knew she was going to make herself.

"I have the afternoon free, so it's no problem," Dorian said, bringing his hands up to his hips as if to demonstrate how physically ready he was.

"Not you," Tara said, shaking her head and dropping a hand on his shoulder. It was a well-muscled shoulder, and one that felt reassuringly solid, but it was still the shoulder of a civilian. "It's too dangerous. I'm sorry. Deputy Grayson and I will climb alone."

Dorian looked disappointed, but he nodded like he was trying to put a brave face on it. "I understand," he said. "I have some climbing equipment in my truck I can lend you."

"That would be appreciated," Tara told him with a smile.

She took a breath as the three of them turned towards the exit. They were really doing this.

They were going up a mountain in search of a killer. A man who was dangerous enough to kill with his hands, strong enough to climb the mountain, maybe on a daily or regular basis. Hardy enough to potentially even live up there by himself.

It was probably crazy to even attempt this. But they had no choice.

There was a killer out there, and it was Tara's sworn duty to stop him – no matter what it cost in personal danger.

# CHAPTER FIFTEEN

He leaned against the pillar outside the general store, looking down the street, pretending he was waiting for someone.

Well, not pretending entirely. He was waiting for someone.

They just didn't know it.

He watched the swarm of people moving backwards and forwards in front of him with mild annoyance. They were like ants. So many of them and seemingly so aimless. All this determined scurrying back and forth, and it mostly amounted to nothing.

It was galling. Irritating. Made him long for the mountain.

But that wasn't the point of him being here. He had to keep trying to remember that. He had a reason to stand out in front of this store and watch the ants moving, and that was because he had one particular ant in mind to watch out for.

The woman scurried on past, and he stood up straighter, watching her go.

It was time.

He stepped out from his spot slowly, casually, checking his watch and his phone as if he was looking at a message from someone telling him to meet them somewhere else or perhaps not to wait anymore. It was a charade, perhaps not terribly convincing, but designed to fool the casual observer.

Not that most of these little scurrying ants ever observed anyone but their own selves. They were all so self-obsessed. So blinkered to everything happening around them. It was part of how he was able to do this so effectively. If any of them thought for a single second in an independent way, there would probably be no chance for him to get them up the mountain in the first place.

He followed at a decent distance as his target moved around, following the same patterns that she often did. Even when there was variation, it was usually easy to predict what someone would do or where they would go after observing them for a while. People were creatures of habit.

Unfortunately, that held true whether the habits were good or bad.

His gaze strayed to the mountain up above the town as he followed his mark through the streets. There it was, their ultimate destination. The other one didn't know it yet, but they would be there soon. He waited and bided his time, following the mark down smaller streets and more isolated places until finally he had the chance to do something.

She was alone then, and he could make his move.

"Excuse me, ma'am," he said as he stepped forward. "I'm going to need you to come with me."

She looked him up and down. "Who are you?"

"I'm a Deputy with the Sheriff's department," he said, gesturing to his body as if to say that the uniform ought to be self-evident.

"Smith?" she frowned, reading his nametag. "There's no Deputy Smith. Not in this town."

Of course. She would be familiar with the local law enforcement. Familiar enough to know them both by name and by sight.

"I'm from Canto Rodado County, ma'am," he told her. "We've been drafted in to help with the search up on the mountains." He knew all about their search efforts. He'd watched them from one of his secret hiding places, saw them begin to swarm out of their vehicles marked with the names of the places they came from. Territorial little ants on his own anthill. Well, it didn't matter to him. Not with the secret things he knew, the things that they didn't know, the things that no one else knew but him.

"What's that got to do with me?" she asked, her jaw jutting out at him. She was a small woman but by God, he could see that she was feisty. "You still don't have jurisdiction to arrest someone out here. Not unless they did a crime in Canto Rodado."

"I'm not arresting you," he said through gritted teeth. Did she have to make this harder than it already was? "I'm asking you to come with me for questioning in relation to a crime. I'll take you to the Sheriff's station in this county. I'm just helping out."

She spat at his feet. "Come back with a warrant," she said.

"Ma'am," he ground out. "This is not a request. It's an order from the Sheriff. You need to come with me."

"I'm not going with no one that wants to try and make me incriminate my boys," she said. "Get a warrant and get a lawyer. I'm not going to that station and you don't have the legal case to force me, or you would have done that in the first place."

Fine. It was time to play this in a way that she would understand. She clearly wasn't ready to listen. He was going to have to do this the opposite way to normal. Start with the threats, not end with them. There was no other way to do it. He had to get her up the mountain, and if he did it by force, it was a very long and hard way to go. He couldn't carry her all that distance, awake or not. "Ma'am," he said, stepping closer. "We have your son in custody right now. And wouldn't you know it, there's a fault with the camera system in the station."

Her gaze tightened. He saw her fist clench around the purse she was holding. "What are you trying to say to me?"

"There are a lot of things that can happen in the holding cell of a Sheriff's station with the cameras off," he said. "Maybe if somebody's mama doesn't want to come in for questioning, we won't bother to go and check on them for a while. Maybe it would be a shame if they tripped and fell and got themselves cut up real bad, and there was no one there to check on them and get them to a doctor."

She looked at him carefully and swallowed.

He had her now. He could see it in her face. It wasn't a matter of if she agreed to come with him, but rather a matter of how.

"Which of my boys you got?" she asked.

"Well, now, Mrs. Weston," he said, using her name just so she knew it wasn't a bluff – so she knew it was real and he knew exactly who she was. "Do you love one of your boys more than the other? If I told you a name, would you think it wasn't worth going in to save them a beating?"

"No," she said, and her voice was resigned. "I love my boys. Doesn't matter which one. Fine. You take me in."

"My car's just this way," he said, gesturing over to the other end of the alley for her to go first.

She wasn't going to try to run. Not now.

The Sheriff thought he was smart, bringing in reinforcements to search the mountain. But he didn't realize one thing. He'd allowed him to hide in plain sight even more. No one was going to question an unfamiliar face on top of a uniform if they knew there were strangers from another county in town.

And absolutely no one was going to question seeing Mrs. Weston get bundled into a car by a Deputy – not with her history and that of her boys. In fact, there was a chance that no one would ever even mention seeing it to the real Sheriff at all, if he ever even knew to ask.

And he had one more person for his mountain, and he already knew she'd go right to the top when he told her to.

# CHAPTER SIXTEEN

Tara looked up at the mountain face above them. It seemed almost sheer. Surely, this wasn't the only way up?

"This is going to be tough," Glenn said, giving rise to her own thoughts.

"You're sure this is it?" Tara asked. She was desperate for him to be wrong. For him to have read the map in some stupid way.

Glenn looked down at the paper again. "This is definitely it," he said. "We have to go up this way."

Tara cursed. She turned and looked back at the way they had come. The town of Wyatt was so small down there, already reduced to a collection of colored splotches – roofs and backyards and streets. The trail until here had been strenuous, and she was already sweating – but the climbing equipment they were carrying on their backs had gone largely unused.

Until now.

Tara wiped a hand across her brow. She could see why Dorian Ball had called this a more challenging climb. Not only was she already getting tired from the length and the steepness of the hike up here, but she could feel the air was thinner as she breathed. It was harder to get enough oxygen into her lungs as she panted for breath, and the heat of the sun overhead wasn't any help, either.

"I'll go up first," Glenn said. He was unpacking things from his backpack, getting ready. "I'll drive these into the rock, make sure you have stable handholds and footholds to follow me with."

"I can come up at the same time as you," Tara said stubbornly. "You don't have to wait for me. I'll climb parallel and we'll be able to get up there at the same time."

Glenn gave her a look. Tara felt herself shrinking just a tiny bit in front of it. He was right; she was a slower climber than him. "Driving these pitons into the rock will slow me down," he said. "There's no point in using extra energy for both of us to do it. You'll be able to keep pace with me easily. Besides, we don't have an unlimited supply. Once these are gone, if we haven't reached the cave yet, we'll have to cling on with crampons and picks – and I don't want to have to do that for a long distance. Not to mention, we still have to get back down again."

Tara sighed. There was no way she could argue with him. He was just right. "Fine," she said. She looked up at the cliff again, wishing she could see the cave.

It was a daunting prospect. The last climb they had done was at a lower altitude with ropes already in place to keep them safe. This time, the only way they were going to have ropes would be once they got to the top and fixed them themselves. And if they fell…

Tara looked back down the mountain at the way they had come. The ledge they were standing on was wide enough not to induce vertigo, but probably not wide enough to guarantee that a fall wouldn't send them right over the edge. If that happened, they would probably bounce half the way to the bottom of the mountain – if they didn't get caught on a tree or a particularly jagged rock. The trail they had walked up wound its way across the mountain face rather than heading straight down; there was no soft landing waiting them anywhere below.

If they fell, it would mean serious injury at the very least – more likely, death.

It was such a short climb in relative terms, but such a dangerous and high one that Tara could almost feel her heart quailing in her chest.

Then she thought about all her colleagues and her sister's team risking their lives across the rest of the mountain, and how they might be able to solve it all by exploring this one cave, and she knew she was going to make this climb no matter what.

Glenn set off first up the face, hammering in the pitons that Dorian Ball had given them, leading the way as he had promised he would. Tara watched restlessly until he was above the height of her head, unable to even start while he was still getting going. When she finally had room to work she stepped onto the lowest pitons, reaching up to grab onto the handholds that Glenn's feet had just left.

Immediately, she realized just how high up she actually was.

Hanging from the rock face, she felt both weightless and far too heavy to be this high up in the air. She glanced over her shoulder as she waited for Glenn to move up. It was a long, long way down. She couldn't even make out much more than the shape of the Sheriff's station down there; people were lost to her, as were the specifics of cars. Glenn moved up another length and Tara followed him, trying to focus on that and hanging on instead of looking down.

They moved up together slowly, almost painfully. Tara found quicker than she had expected that she was no longer really waiting for

Glenn between moves; his actions at driving the pitons into the rock got quicker, while hers stayed the same, hauling herself up cautiously each time a piton was free.

Once she was high enough to know that a fall would hurt, Tara hugged the rock even closer, praying for her muscles not to seize up and drop her to the ground below.

Even though the sun was hot, it was cooler up here. The wind was stronger, tugging at her hair and the folds of her clothes. She stopped looking around, even looking up, and made it a game of focusing completely on the next step ahead. She looked only to see where her next handhold was, reaching for the piton below with her foot, remembering the old positions of her body to guide herself towards it more easily. Glenn's placement was evenly spaced out, making it more convenient to keep moving her arms and legs in the same method.

Then he stopped, and for a heart-stopping moment Tara thought that something must be wrong. That he was stuck or he would fall. But she looked up and saw him leaning down to look back at her, hands still clenched firmly onto pitons so that he wouldn't slip.

"We're at the top," he told her in a low voice. She didn't know how much point there was in staying quiet. The noise of their climb ought to have been audible to anyone in the cave. But that just made it all the more important that they proceed with caution.

"Go slow," Tara told him. "Have your gun ready."

She tried not to think about what would happen if the killer was up there waiting – if he simply pushed Glenn back over the edge – if Glenn took her out as he fell…

They didn't have a special mountaineering unit. Not here in Edgar County. The mountaineering crew was just the people in the Sheriff's department who were trained to climb. Glenn, Alonzo, Kay, Walker. There were a few EMTs trained for mountain rescue, but no chance they would be included in a law enforcement search like this one – a search where the suspect could be armed and, even if not, was certainly dangerous. There was a helicopter crew on standby, but not every part of the mountain was accessible that way, and it depended on the weather.

It was a good enough day. If they needed to call for help, they were likely to get it. But that was only if either of them still had the strength – or the cell service – to make the call.

Tara told herself again not to think about that as Glenn raised his head over the ledge at the top of the cliff, moving slowly and cautiously.

He climbed up over the edge almost silently, and Tara scrambled to follow him without getting caught up in his legs. Once she joined him over the edge she could see where they had landed more clearly, scanning her eyes around rapidly for any sign of movement or life.

There were none, but she remained wary as she caught her breath, crouching on the ledge that created the entrance to the cave. It was a more or less flat surface leaving them enough room to stand, walk around a few paces, and sit, but little else than that. The mouth of the cave was wide and gaping, though it had a slight overhang ahead that must have protected it from some of the elements.

Glenn caught her attention with a wave of his hand and then jerked his chin towards the cave – a question. Tara nodded but held up a hand for a moment, reaching to free her gun from its holster. They didn't know if they were alone here, and the mountain still rose above and around them. A good climber who knew the secret ways to get up here could be anywhere around them, waiting to strike.

Then she dropped her hand and they both proceeded forward, walking into the cave with their eyes as wide open as possible and their heads swiveling in all directions in search of any sign of someone there.

Inside the cave, it was calmer. The wind was not as strong, and a hazy warmth permeated the first few feet until they reached the cooler rock behind. It was quiet without the sound of the wind, almost eerily so.

The inside of the cave was curious. Mostly bare and clear, almost as if this was a place that had been carved out of the rock by human hands. Tara could understand it on one level: at some time, a vast river must have formed a pool here, rushing over the edge of the cliff in a waterfall that smoothed away some of the surfaces they had climbed. It might even have been the same water that carved the hiking trail down the mountain's face, a meandering spiral that allowed them to reach the ground safely.

On another level, it felt like being in some kind of mystical space carved by alien forces – or by cavemen eons ago with nothing more than their hands and other rocks.

After a tense few moments, Tara lowered her gun. "It's empty," she said, hearing her voice bounce back to her against the rock at the back of the cave. That was a good sign. If there was any movement they had missed, they would hear it.

"There's some stuff over here," Glenn replied, holstering his own firearm. "Looks like camping gear."

Alarm flared again in Tara's chest. She walked past him, directly towards the items he had spotted. Was it possible that the killer had been living here, after all?

But – no; the gear, as Glenn had called it, looked old. Very old. Like it hadn't been touched or used in a long while. There was a sleeping bag that seemed moth-eaten, full of holes and smeared with what Tara quickly realized was some kind of animal excrement. There were old food wrappers that were long empty, stuffed against the wall behind a rock, presumably so the wind couldn't take them. Looking closer as she squatted down, Tara saw they were piled on top of what might have once been clothes, now mostly scraps of fabric.

"This brand," Tara said, pointing towards the chip packet on the top of the pile, not quite touching anything yet. "Didn't they discontinue that?"

Glenn squatted beside her, resting on his haunches. "Yeah, I remember those," he said. "We used to get them when I was a kid. I haven't seen them in… I don't know. I'd say at least ten years."

Tara chewed her lower lip. Those chips… she was sure she remembered seeing Cassie eating the same brand in the week before she went missing. She'd spent so much time going over and over those days in her head, and Cassie had liked that flavor. Surely…

"This isn't our killer," Tara said out loud. "Whoever was using this as a place to sleep did it years ago. Maybe back when those chips were last manufactured." She took a pair of gloves out of one of her pockets and began snapping them onto her hands, wiggling her fingers to get the tight plastic to fit her hands better.

"It's not evidence, is it?" Glenn asked.

"Maybe not for this case," Tara said thoughtfully. "If someone was sleeping up here, they had a reason. And we do still have a number of missing persons cases left open from back then. Who knows – we might get lucky with a DNA hit and have another piece of the story."

Tara felt rather than saw Glenn staring at the back of her head. Felt him turning it over in his own mind, thinking about missing persons cases from a decade ago. Putting the dots together.

"Okay," he said, and the tone in his voice was different. "Yeah, that's a good idea. Have you got enough evidence bags with you? I have some in my pocket."

"I should be good," Tara said. She put the strange note of his voice out of her head. Of course, he figured out that Cassie was a good match for that timeframe. Of course, he went straight to sympathy. Of course, he didn't say it out loud because he didn't want to upset her.

Never mind that even the avoidance of the subject itself was enough to remind her of how raw the loss still was, would always be, until she knew what had happened to her sister.

She stuffed the empty food wrappers into one evidence bag and then each of the pieces of clothing into another; she thought she could identify a shirt, sweater, and perhaps pants or a skirt, but the fabric was so old and half-rotted that it was crumbling as she lifted it. She sealed each bag carefully and slipped them into the backpack she was wearing, reaching over her own shoulder to manage the zipper.

"We should go," she said, standing up and glancing around. Glenn had wandered towards the back of the cave. "There's nothing else here."

"No, I don't think so," Glenn agreed. "Just some fresh dung over here."

Tara lifted her head. "How fresh?"

"I'm not going to touch it, but it almost looks like it could be warm," Glenn said. "Part of some kind of dead animal here, too. Maybe a bird or a rodent or something; it's small."

Tara's heart thudded in her chest. "We should leave," she said, all the alarm bells going off in her head at once. "We don't know what left that or when it's coming back."

"Yeah," Glenn said, turning back towards the mouth of the cave. "Let's -"

And he cut himself off at the same time a growl reverberated through the cave, turning Tara's bones to jelly.

# CHAPTER SEVENTEEN

Glenn's first instinct was sheer and unutterable panic.

"Get out of the cave," Tara told him, her voice low and urgent. "We have to get out of the cave."

"It's blocking the entrance," he hissed back at her, unable to take his eyes off the mountain lion that was staring right back at them with its hackles raised.

"She's warning us," Tara said. "This is her den. We need to get out. Come to my side."

Glenn rapidly crossed the cave to stand beside Tara, all too happy to find what little safety there was in numbers. "Then what?"

"Follow my lead," Tara said. She looked calm. So calm Glenn could barely believe it. But he saw a bead of sweat at her hairline and he knew she was just as panicked inside as he was.

He wasn't sure whether that was reassuring, or the opposite.

Tara started to slowly step forward, crossing one leg over the other rather than walking straight, keeping her arms out to the sides and open. A gesture of peace – showing the lion that she was not armed, that she didn't want to hurt her. Glenn thought about his gun. Couldn't he take out his gun? But Tara knew what she was doing. She was calm and rational, and Glenn copied her movements as they stepped towards the furthest right-hand-side of the cave mouth.

The lion growled at them, baring its teeth, stepping around to the left with long, prowling, slow strides as if matching their pace.

They were almost out of the cave. The ledge wasn't very wide, but at least they didn't have their backs to a wall.

Not that having their backs to a sheer drop all the way down a mountain was much better.

"Easy," Tara murmured, stepping out onto the ledge slowly. "Easy. Don't spook her."

"We're not going to be able to put a rope in," Glenn said. "We can't use tools. She'll lunge for us."

"It's okay," Tara said, keeping her voice calm and low like he was a horse that needed soothing. "We'll just climb down nice and steady. It's going to be fine."

There was a mewing kind of sound somewhere to the left, just as they stepped out onto the ledge together, and Glenn froze, his gaze following the noise.

Two mountain lion cubs were picking their way down the rock, following their mother.

Everything happened so quickly.

Tara swore under her breath. Glenn reached towards the gun on his belt, and Tara's arm snapped out, hitting his hand. He fumbled and dropped the gun and heard it clatter to the ground, miraculously not going off. The mountain lion lunged back towards them, growling wildly, launching herself between them and her cubs.

And now they were all out on the ledge together, and the family of mountain lions was between Tara and Glenn and the pitons they had driven into the rock on the way up.

"Stay still," Tara ordered him, her voice taut and driven through gritted teeth, her hands still out to the sides and in front of him. "Don't move."

"But," Glenn started, wanting to protest. She had knocked his gun down. It hadn't landed well. He dared a glance at the ground and saw it wedged halfway down the side of the cliff, against an outcropping of rock that was far too far away to reach.

"No," Tara said. "If you point a gun at her, we're done. There's no way we get off enough shots to bring her down or accurately hit her while she's jumping at us. We'd be done."

"Then what?" Glenn hissed furiously. He was on the verge of sheer, windmill-tilting, mad-risk-taking, cliff-jumping panic.

"Maintain eye contact with her," Tara said. "We move slow and calm like we just did. Show her we're not out to get her. Let her get into the safety of the cave. Then we just have to climb down one by one, nice and slow."

Glenn swallowed. He didn't know anything about surviving mountain lion encounters. He'd been given some kind of briefing on it when he was doing his climbing training but he didn't remember a single word of it now. Though what Tara had said seemed to ring true. He just had to trust her.

"Just back away a little bit," Tara said, moving a foot slowly backwards. "Show her we don't mean anything bad."

Glenn did as he was told, sliding his feet backwards, keeping his arms up like Tara was, keeping his eyes on the mountain lion. On her, not the cubs. A small pebble skittered away from his foot and he glanced down. Not far from the edge.

The mountain lion stalked forward, keeping pace with them, pushing them further back.

Glenn's foot slid backwards and found air, making him stop dead.

"Tara," he whispered. "I'm at the edge."

She didn't say anything. They paused right there for a moment, almost hanging in time. The mountain lion growled and took another step towards them.

Then another.

Glenn looked over his shoulder. There was nothing but air behind them, nothing until a particularly jagged outcrop of the mountain so many feet below he knew there was no way anyone was going to survive that fall.

They were going to die.

Glenn looked up at the mountain lion again. She was still growling, baring her teeth, her eyes focused on Tara like she was getting ready to leap. The cubs behind her were quiet, watching their mama at work. Protecting them. Glenn couldn't even blame her. They'd walked right into her home.

Glenn tried to run through the scenarios. At the very least, the mountain lion was going to lunge for one of them. Maybe the other would be able to make a break for it. Head for the pitons and somehow manage to climb far enough down to get away from the mountain lion's reach. How far could she swipe with those heavy paws? How well could she climb a sheer cliff face? How did she get up here, anyway?

One of them, at the very least, was going to die. Glenn simply couldn't see a scenario where it didn't happen. And even if one of them occupied the mountain lion, the chances of the other managing to climb back down the sheer cliff face with no harness support under such stress and pressure was low.

This could be it.

"Tara," Glenn said urgently. "I need you to know something."

"Now's not the time, Glenn," Tara replied firmly, keeping her eyes on the mountain lion. She was still advancing. Any minute now, Glenn thought, and she leaps.

"It's the only time," he argued. "Tara, if we don't make it out of here, I can't bear the thought that I didn't tell you."

"What, then?" Tara asked, almost sounding impatient.

"I…" Glenn swallowed. "I have feelings for you."

There was a heartbeat of silence. Glenn could swear even the mountain lion looked stunned.

“Tara?” he prompted. He wanted her to say something. Anything. To indicate she had heard him. To tell him she had feelings, too, most of all. To throw it all to the damn wind and turn around and kiss him while the mountain lion pounced. Why the hell not, if they were going to die anyway?

“I can’t deal with this right now, Glenn,” Tara said, her voice tight. “I… this is too much. I have to focus.”

Glenn’s heart dropped like a stone into his stomach, along with everything else.

He wasn’t just going to die. He was going to die feeling rejected.

The mountain lion didn’t seem to like them talking to one another at all. She took two more rapid paces forward and stared at them angrily. She was so close now. Close enough to spring, Glenn thought, watching the muscles bunch in her limbs. His foot skated backward just a little on its own and he felt air under his heel again. One more moment and she was going to pounce. She was going to take them both out at once and drag them down the side of the mountain, and probably chew their bones until there was nothing left.

A light flashed in her eyes as she bunched her muscles even further, and –

The sound of a loud horn blasted in the air right above them, so loud Glenn flinched and almost tumbled back down the mountain on his own accord. The mountain lion turned, her muscles bunched in another direction now as she almost chased her own tail, staring up as if to see where the noise was coming from. She made another growl and lunged for her babies, grabbing one of them by the neck and bounding deep into the cave as the other cub ran after her.

“Up here!” someone shouted, and Glenn had never been so grateful to hear a human voice in his life.

“There,” Tara said, gesturing to him, and Glenn looked to see someone standing somehow up what looked like an impassible part of the side of the mountain, way above their heads to the left of the cave entrance, where the mountain lion and her cubs must have jumped from. Tara rushed forward and Glenn was right behind her, sparing only one glance to see the animals bunched together at the back of the cave, reflective eyes glaring back out at him and sending a chill down his spine.

The rescuer, whoever it was, leaned down and grasped Tara by the forearm, helping her to scramble up the loose rocks, somehow managing to leap up to the top of the formation, where it was apparently stable ground. Glenn rushed close behind her, reaching up for that same helping hand, soon finding himself panting beside Tara on the rock ledge that formed the top of the cave's entrance.

"We can't hang around here for long," someone said – and Glenn caught his breath and brought his mind back down to earth enough to realize that their rescuer was Tara's sister, Jessy, and the partner she'd set off to climb with. She was holding a bright red air horn in one hand. "That lion'll be out soon, prowling and making sure we're not threatening her cubs. Come on – there's a climb route a few hundred feet over the other side of this ledge."

Glenn followed at the back of the group as they hastily scrambled to return to the spot where Jessy had climbed to reach a higher cave, a route they hadn't realized before would connect to the cave they had been investigating. So little up here was mapped out. His legs felt numb. He was probably in shock, he guessed, his brain still trying to work out if he was actually alive or dead.

And he stared at the back of Tara's head, rushing forward right behind her sister, never once looking back for him.

And he already knew in his gut that he'd made a mistake.

He was light-headed, unsteady, and he almost tripped on a small rock that was scattered across the path as they moved to the descent. Jessy made Tara go first, standing by to usher down her partner from Canto Rodado County and then Glenn, letting them go down the single file climb before her. Glenn's legs were so shaky he wondered if he was even going to make it down. The Sheriff had managed to hammer a rope into place, something to keep them steady as they climbed down, a connection they could harness to, and Glenn was glad. He knew without it he would be too afraid of falling down the mountain.

All the way down the climb, he kept asking himself the same question.

Did he feel so unstable because they had faced a near-death experience and the adrenaline was still flooding through his body?

Because of all the physical difficulties of climbing, the strain, and the inherent danger it posed?

Or because he had a horrible, sinking feeling that he had just forever destroyed the friendship he cherished with Tara – because there was no chance she actually liked him back?

# CHAPTER EIGHTEEN

During the ride back to the Sheriff's station, Tara opted for staring straight ahead. That, coincidentally, turned out to give her a view of the whole street ahead of them and not a glimpse at all of Glenn, or Jessy's partner sitting beside him in the back seat.

Jessy swung the steering wheel down the turnoff for the station, glancing sideways at her sister as she did so. "I don't know why you didn't have an air horn with you," she said.

Tara couldn't even find it in herself to be annoyed at the criticism. Jessy was right, anyway. They'd gone up there unprepared. That was why they had gotten themselves into such a dangerous situation. If they had stopped to prepare better, they would have been fine. In fact, Tara wondered even why Dorian Ball hadn't brought up the need to take some kind of deterrent with them.

"Next time, I will," she said distantly. There were a lot of cars parked out front of the station. As Jessy pulled up to a stop, Tara bit her lip, wondering if any of the other returned search parties would have anything to report.

"Next time, maybe just let me do the climbing," Jessy said. She switched off the engine and her voice softened for just a moment as she reached out to rest a hand on top of Tara's. "Little sister."

Tara looked up to smile at her, to let her know the sentiment hadn't gone unnoticed, but Jessy was already getting out of the car and heading towards the building. Tara sighed and did the same, unbuckling herself and getting out of her seat. Somehow it felt that all of her movements were far too slow since the mountain lion. Like she was stuck in a state of shock.

"Tara," Glenn said quietly, materializing at her side, and Tara bit her lip and looked at the station ahead of them.

She had nothing to say. She didn't know where to go with it. What he'd said had been so unexpected, so out of left field. They were partners. That was all they had ever been. Friends, too, yes, but – more? She'd had no idea he had any kind of feelings for her at all, and to hear it in that setting, to feel like everything was going to end and then see a rescue at the last minute…

“I, um,” she said, and Glenn dropped his eyes to the ground.

“I’m sorry,” he said. His ears were turning pink. “I shouldn’t have said anything. It was – I was just caught up in the moment. Forget about it.”

“No,” Tara blurted out, but found again she had nothing to back it up with. She didn’t know what to say. She could see Glenn was embarrassed, but she didn’t want his declaration to just float away on the wind as if it meant nothing to either of them. There was something wrong about that. With all the respect she had for him, with how much it must have meant to him to say it, she had to deal with it, somehow. She just didn’t know how. Or when. Or what. “I mean – I…”

“It’s fine,” Glenn said. He was staring steadfastly at a particular spot on the parking lot floor, a white line dividing spaces, as if it was important somehow. “Let’s just forget I said anything.”

“I don’t want to forget it,” Tara said, and the hope in Glenn’s eyes when he looked up was almost painful. She took a deep breath. “But I can’t talk about it right now. Not with all of this going on. I need to focus on the case.”

Glenn swallowed and nodded quickly. “It’s an important case,” he said, hope and disappointment warring for control of his voice. He wore his heart so much on his sleeve, she had no idea how she hadn’t spotted this before his confession.

“When it’s solved,” she said, feeling marginally better about the decision the more she solidified it. “Then we’ll talk.”

Glenn nodded again and looked at the building in front of them rapidly. The pink was spreading from his ears to his cheeks. “We should get inside,” he said, a rough edge to his voice. Tara thought that maybe he couldn’t stand the embarrassment anymore. She followed a few steps behind him as they entered their familiar workplace.

Noise hit them as they entered the building – noise coming from the open doors of the office up ahead, where all the deputies must have been gathering. Tara nodded to a slightly beleaguered-looking Tracy behind the front desk; Tracy made a mark on a piece of paper with a serious look and then nodded back.

“You’re the last ones to come back,” she informed them, which sounded to Tara a lot like saying no one else had found anything either. If they had, surely, Sheriff Braddock would have called them back.

The hubbub was only louder as they entered the room, which was packed to the rafters with deputies from both counties. At the front of the room, near the briefing board and the map they had used earlier, the two Sheriffs were already deep in conversation. Tara glanced around, snippets of conversation catching her ears. Shared stories about climbs and hikes, about the weather, the things they had seen and people they had encountered. Tara figured they were probably the only ones who could count a mountain lion among that figure.

"Alright," Sheriff Braddock said, holding up a hand to get everyone's attention. He'd shouted to call their eyes to him, but every other voice in the room went quiet, allowing him to continue at normal volume. "We now have everyone back here present and accounted for. What I understand is that no one found anything relevant to the case. Is that correct?"

He glanced around pointedly, spending a couple of seconds looking at Tara. She lowered her eyes to the floor. She'd wasted time and managed to come up with absolutely nothing. He was probably disappointed in her. If he wasn't, he should have been.

"Are we going back out again?" one of the Canto Rodado County deputies spoke up.

"No, I don't think that's a good idea tonight," Sheriff Braddock said. "At least, not to climb. I'll need about half of you, or slightly less, to volunteer for some evening work. I'll have you posted in pairs at the entrances to some of the trail spots – places where a person would be most likely to start up the mountain. It's getting close to evening, and within a very short amount of time it's going to be far too dangerous to have anyone up on that mountain in any capacity. We just can't risk it. I understand one of our parties already had a close encounter with the local wildlife that could have ended very badly, and that risk as well as all the others gets magnified in the dark."

All of the eyes in the room swung towards Tara and Glenn along with the Sheriff's gesture in their direction. Tara shifted uncomfortably and tried to look as unaffected as possible. She raised her chin just to show them that she was fine, that being stared at was nothing.

"What about the rest of us?" she asked, out loud, shifting the attention back to Sheriff Braddock.

"A bit of rest is in order," he said. "We may need to conduct a similar search tomorrow. This map only accounts for the known and mapped caves on that mountain; from what we know, there could be many more on faces that are a little harder to climb. I'd like everyone to report back here tomorrow morning, first thing, so we can allocate routes and tasks."

The others nodded, murmuring, and shifting among themselves. Tara wasn't satisfied.

There was no way she was going home to rest. She'd done that last night, and another victim had shown up dead.

People were starting to move. Glenn turned to Tara with a regretful look on his face, and for a horrible moment she thought he was going to try to bring up something related to his confession again.

"I take it there's no way I can convince you to go home and sleep, is there?" he said.

Tara bit the inside of her cheek but was unsuccessful in holding back a smile. "No," she said. "There isn't."

"Alright," Glenn said with a resigned shake of his head. "What are we doing?"

"We have no new leads," she sighed. "I think we have to go back over what we already have. Make sure we haven't missed anything." She glanced at the Sheriff; he was busy talking to the volunteers who were staying behind for the night watch. The only people who were leaving were the older deputies, like Collins, and a couple of the ones she knew had young families. From the age distribution of those leaving from the Canto Rodado side, she figured it was the same for them as well.

"I'll get the case files laid out across our desks," Glenn said, because he knew how Tara liked to work.

"I'll join you in a minute," she said. She still had her backpack at her side, and she hefted it up to grab the evidence bags she had placed inside. "I'm going to go see if Lindsie is still in the lab."

She headed off down the hall again, past Tracy, and towards the building next door that housed both the county morgue and Lindsie's lab.

Maybe this stuff was nothing. But it was worth running it through the lab to see if any DNA came up – especially if, like Tara, Lindsie was wired and nervous and needed something to do. If she was still snowed under with other work from the current case, it could wait until after.

Tara looked down at the items in her hands as she entered the lab, glancing around and spotting Lindsie bending over what looked like a crossword puzzle at her desk. Chip packets, candy wrappers, torn and rotten old clothing. Was it something, or nothing? With a family of mountain lions taking up residence, this was probably close to the only evidence that cave was ever going to divulge.

Maybe it was nothing. But if there was any slim chance it could be linked to another unsolved case and give solace to the families of the missing or dead, Tara knew from firsthand experience that the family would most likely donate all their right arms to hear about it.

"Hi, Lindsie," she said, calling their forensic specialist's attention and giving her a smile, then holding the evidence bags out for her to see.

***

Tara walked back into the Sheriff's office to find it a much quieter place. Almost everyone was gone; only Glenn, standing over their joined desks with his arms leaning on the side, and one deputy left to man the phones – Bryant, who drew the short straw often by being the youngest and newest member of the team. He was sitting in silence, playing a card game on his phone, and leaning back in his chair while he waited for the tipline to ring.

"What do we have?" Tara asked, standing opposite Glenn on the other side of the desks. She tried not to psychoanalyze herself and what it meant that she felt safest with a whole two desks of physical space separating them now.

"I'm having a hard time seeing anything new," Glenn said. "What we have is what we already know. The killer likes to strike on the mountains at night, and he's killed two people now by hitting them over the head."

"Or hitting their head into the ground," Tara reminded him. She glanced over at the windows; someone had closed all the blinds before leaving, but she knew full well that it was dark out there now. Perfect for the killer. Right on time for them to stop searching for him so he could strike.

"And the only connection we have between the two of them so far is this climbing instructor, Dorian Ball, who checks out clean for the night that Kimmie Hutson was murdered."

"Did they check his alibi?" Tara asked. She had been so caught up in the climb and search of the mountain, she hadn't even thought to ask.

Glenn lifted a page of information from the file. "Your sister has a couple of guys back in Canto Rodado making calls. Looks like yes. They were able to verify with the troop leader for the Scouts that he relieved Dorian for second watch that night exactly as planned, and Dorian hadn't moved from his spot in front of their little campfire, wrapped up in a blanket."

Tara sighed. It wasn't that she had wanted Dorian to be guilty, or even truly suspected it to be the case. Then again, he had sent them on a wild goose chase to that cave – though she did believe his intentions were good. She just wished they had *something*.

"We should talk to him again in the morning," she said. "Maybe there's a client of his who has been taking lessons for years – someone who would have come across both of the victims at times when they were learning. Or maybe it would have been his assistant – that woman who gave you all of the information."

Glenn shook his head. "They looked into her, too. She started working with him after Kimmie would have done her lessons."

Tara looked at the closed window again, biting her lip. She didn't need to open the blinds to see the view; she'd seen it so many times. On that side of the building, the windows gave a clear view of the mountain, looming in the near distance. She thought about those slopes and cliffs and how perilous it would be to climb them right now, in the dark. Still. She had an itch, a temptation to go out there.

Bryant's phone rang and he answered it, a buzz at the back of Tara's attention. She tried to focus on some kind of train of thought that would lead her in the right direction – something she could use to form a course of action.

"And you last saw her when?"

Tara's attention swung back sharply to Deputy Bryant with those words.

"Okay. And that's unusual for her? Right. Have you tried calling her?"

Tara made her way over to Bryant's side, peering over his shoulder at his notepad. He had written down the name of the woman that the caller was apparently reporting as missing. *Sara Weston*.

Sara was the mother of the Weston boys, the family who caused a lot of trouble in Wyatt. Just on the last major case, Tara had ended up questioning Tim as a possible suspect. On that occasion, he'd only been guilty of misogyny, but he and his brother Donny had been involved in plenty more things over the years.

Sara Weston was missing. Now, Tara had to wonder who in their right mind would think that the mother of the Weston boys was a good target for a kidnapping.

Because if they didn't find her, there was a strong chance that those boys would take justice into their own hands – and if she wasn't a victim of their killer but simply off somewhere else, there was going to be a reckoning without justification.

But on the other hand…

If she was a victim of the killer, then Tara needed to act fast. She didn't want to find another body in the morning, and the fact it was a Weston would only make the whole case harder to handle.

She waited impatiently for Bryant to finish his call, needing to know any tiny clue they had that might lead them to her – because as things stood, they had nothing at all to help them predict the killer's movements or who he might be.

# CHAPTER NINETEEN

Tara slapped the printed photograph up on their briefing wall, feeling it stick as she took her hand away.

"Sara Weston," she said out loud, turning to Glenn. "Anything from your calls?"

He shook his head. "No one saw anything weird when she left work today."

"Nothing from the rest of the family, either," Tara said with a sigh. "Both Weston boys are accounted for. Her husband's going out of his mind. Poor Bryant."

"Poor husband," Glenn said with more feeling. "We haven't had any reports of movement back from the teams watching the most common trails, so if the killer does have her, they're not taking an obvious route."

"Sara isn't as agile as the first two victims would have been," Tara said thoughtfully, looking at the cave map. "Could he really be making her climb up the side of the mountain, with proper gear? It seems too risky."

Glenn shook his head unknowingly. "Maybe he has a route we don't know about. An easier climb but out of the way of our watches."

Tara sighed, trying to think. There was no official confirmation yet that Sara actually had been abducted; for all they knew, she had simply gone to a bar on the way home and forgotten to tell her husband. Her phone was off, but that could have been a signal issue or even due to lack of battery. Or maybe she had just finally walked out on her difficult family and didn't want them to find her.

No, that couldn't be it. There was one thing the Westons had going for them, and that was loyalty. Sara loved her sons too much to just walk away, no matter how much trouble they were likely to get into.

"I need to check out the place where she should have last been seen," Tara said. She tapped the large map of Wyatt township that was always taped up on the back wall of the office. "Her husband said she was popping to the store after work and then should have been walking straight home. I'll walk the route with a flashlight and see what comes up."

"I'll come with you," Glenn said, moving towards his desk to grab his jacket.

"No," Tara said, maybe a little too quickly. "No – I need to clear my head and try to get some clarity on this case. Try and see Sara Weston without seeing the killer, make sure I'm not just conflating two things that aren't related. It's best if I go alone."

"Right," Glenn said, his shoulders sagging a little. "I'll… I'll stay here."

"Go home and get some rest," Tara said. It was meant to come off as sympathetic. "Bryant's always here if I need to call for urgent backup."

From the way Glenn's shoulders slumped even more as he nodded, Tara knew she had come across as cruel, not kind.

She took a breath but used it to grab her jacket and head for the doors of the office, not to try to fix things. She had the feeling that even if she did try, she would only end up saying the wrong thing.

"Oh, hey, Deputy Sheriff," someone called out to her. She looked up, seeing Deputy Kay coming towards her. The young Deputy, part of the climbing team, was holding what looked like a harness in his hands. He tossed it onto the desk where Tracy normally sat, though she was gone for the night now. "Someone told me you were climbing earlier."

Tara nodded. "Glenn and I," she said.

"Did you get extra gear? We're out in the supply closet."

"We borrowed some from a local climbing instructor," Tara said. "Why?"

Kay gestured towards his discarded harness, his face rueful. "One of the straps is about close to wearing through. It's not fit for use up on the mountain tonight if I need to go after a suspect. I'm supposed to be guarding the steepest trail and I don't want to risk having to watch him get away. Can I borrow yours?"

Tara nodded, gesturing outside. "Come on. I'll take you to the car."

The night air hit her in the face like a blast, chilling her to the bone. Tara zipped her jacket up quickly and hurried to the trunk of the car she and Glenn had been using earlier, finding, and grabbing Glenn's pack. Kay thanked her and jogged off to his own vehicle with the new harness in his hand, with Tara making a mental note to get it back from him in the morning so it would be returned to Dorian Ball in one piece.

Tara locked up the car and grabbed her flashlight from her belt. The Sheriff's station was on the outskirts of town, but Wyatt itself wasn't a huge place. It would take such a short time to get to the alleged site of

Sara Weston's disappearance that there was no point in taking a car at all.

Plus, she really did need the walk to clear her head.

Not to spend time thinking about Glenn's confession and how she felt about it. No, that was something that truly was going to have to wait until the case was over. In the meantime, the unfortunate thing was that it had created distance between them. She couldn't rely on him like she usually did. Couldn't ask him to do things for her or push the boundaries of their working schedule with her, because if he was doing it as a result of his feelings rather than regard for the case, she was taking advantage.

And then there was all the rest of it. Jessy. Having her come into Tara's own county and walk around like she was in charge. Tara knew that Jessy was doing a good thing by coming to help, and that she was doing what she could in her own way to show her support. The thing was that Jessy's own way was awkward, abrasive, and often calculated to do more harm than good, at least on a personal level. Tara didn't need all the reminders of how inadequate she was compared to her older sister.

Now Jessy had gone home, anyway, leaving some of her men to help keep watch. She hadn't even said goodbye to Tara. That was par for the course. But it meant Tara had lost yet another opportunity to talk with her about the possibility of reopening Cassie's case. When would they next have a chance to talk? If Jessy didn't come tomorrow, or she did but the work kept them apart, it might be weeks before their paths crossed again. All the while, the guilt about not telling her what she was thinking was going to eat away at Tara.

Tara shoved her hands deeper into the pockets of her jacket against the chill, letting her feet take her along the long street that led to the place where Sara Weston worked. There was hardly anyone around. Not only was it less busy around here in the first place after dark, but she had no doubt that people were choosing to stay home to stay off the streets and away from whoever was taking people up the mountain to die. Tara hadn't caught the local news today, but by now it was surely all over the place that two people were dead in suspicious circumstances. That was the kind of thing that got people talking.

She had to focus, concentrate. Had to get all this stuff out of her mind and think about Sara Weston.

The streetlights above illuminated the place where she would have stepped outside of her workplace. Tara glanced up and down the street and made a quick examination of the ground. It was too busy out here.

If she was taken here, someone would have seen her, unless, of course, there was some trick the killer had for getting them to come quietly. Even so, there would be a risk of witnesses. He surely had to strike somewhere else.

Tara followed the most direct route from here to the store that Deputy Bryant had noted down in his call. They would have to establish somehow whether Sara Weston had made it inside or not, whether she had made a purchase. They could use credit card records and interview the staff, but it was too late tonight; the place was closed, everyone gone home. In the morning it could help narrow things down. For now, Tara swept the beam of her flashlight left to right across the ground between streetlights, looking for any sign of something that might indicate a struggle. A broken necklace or a dropped earring, a ripped piece of fabric, groceries abandoned, or a purse lying on the side of the road – even a bit of scuffed up earth beside the sidewalk. But there was nothing.

"Searching for something?"

Tara almost jumped out of her own skin, turning around with a curse to shine her flashlight into the face of the person who had called out to her. She knew the voice, but seeing the face helped to settle her nerves. It was Lydia Peablossom, the town's resident gossip, who had no doubt taken it upon herself to look around for any sign of an update.

"Ms. Peablossom," Tara said, taking in the large woman's embroidered velvet coat and the curls of her old-fashioned hairstyle. "It's late for you to be out."

Lydia made a vague noise of agreement, glancing at the floor and scuffing it with one ballet-pump foot as if she was totally innocent and had a very good reason to be out at night. "I just wondered if you were looking for something. What Sara Weston was doing over here earlier, maybe."

Tara raised an eyebrow, walking right over to the older woman. "What makes you think that?"

"Well, I saw her getting into a car with your deputy on the way home from the store," Lydia shrugged. "Did she drop some evidence that might be helpful? Is that what you're thinking?"

Tara stared at her for a long moment. There was no record of Sara Weston being taken in with a deputy – if she had been, it would have flagged during Bryant's initial call. Besides, almost all the Sheriff's staff had been up on the mountain all day. "Which deputy?" she asked at last.

"Oh, I don't know," Lydia said, waving a hand – which was a cause for concern in itself. "One of the Canto Rodado boys, I should expect. I thought I recognized him, though I can't place him. Someone's son, I think."

Canto Rodado? No – every single member of the Canto Rodado team had been climbing. Sure, some of them had come back early, but they'd gone straight back to the Sheriff's office. Right?

"Thank you, Ms. Peablossom," Tara said. "You ought to get on home, now. It's not as safe as it used to be out here after dark."

Lydia took the cryptic hint as manna from heaven, like Tara had known she would – an ostensibly innocent comment that would set Lydia's gossip wheels into overdrive. The woman beamed and turned to hurry away, though her usual pace was significantly slower than Tara would have liked.

Tara bit her lip, thinking. She began to set off back along the street, returning to the more populated areas of town. On the way, she pulled her cell phone out of her pocket and dialed her own desk phone, knowing it would divert through to Bryant.

"Hello, Edgar County Sheriff's Department," Byrant said. "How can I help?"

"Bryant, it's me," Tara replied. "Can you check something for me? Is anyone logged as talking to or bringing in Sara Weston earlier today?"

"No," Bryant said immediately. She could hear his fingers on the keyboard all the same. "No, like I said. There's nothing. I would have seen that when I first checked."

"I just had to be sure," Tara said. "Say – she doesn't have any outstanding warrants in Canto Rodado County?"

There was the sound of more typing. "No, nothing on the system."

"Alright." Tara thought for a minute. "Bryant, I need you to be on the alert for any sightings or reports that come in involving a deputy. You haven't heard anything like that over the last few days, have you?"

"What do you mean?" Bryant asked.

Tara was coming back under the streetlights of Main Street. She didn't want to say too much in a place where she could be overheard, without knowing for sure if she was right. There was always a chance that Lydia had been mistaken somehow – that she'd seen someone in khaki or just another kind of uniform and got it wrong. "Like a deputy seen talking to one of our missing victims, or sniffing around the scenes before they went missing, that kind of thing."

"No," Bryant said, sounding totally mystified. "Nothing like that at all."

"Alright. Thanks," Tara said. "Just stay alert, like I said. It sounds like a deputy spoke with Weston earlier today, but I have yet to confirm. I'll tell you more when I know."

She hung up the phone, wanting to get off the line and keep her wits about her. There was no telling what danger lurked on these dark streets right now.

She stopped in the center of town, more or less, and looked around. Something was going on here, but she wasn't sure she understood what. She sat down on one of the stone benches that lined a small memorial square, feeling the cold of the structure through her clothes but needing to sit and think more than she needed to be warm.

Was it possible that someone was masquerading as a deputy in order to get people to go with them?

That comment Lydia had made about 'someone's son' needed more analysis, but maybe she could get her in tomorrow to make a witness statement. In the meantime, Tara needed to follow this through. She could see a uniform being helpful for getting someone in a car, for example, or asking them to follow you a short distance – but up the mountain? The killer would still need a different method for that.

What could he be doing?

Was the uniform just a way to hide in plain sight? A way to abduct people without any screaming or fuss, without anyone spotting them and finding it suspicious? People weren't likely to come forward as witnesses if they thought the Sheriff had already been involved.

Was that it? Just a disguise to help him carry out what he wanted to do without being noticed?

That made Tara think deeper. Someone who operated in the shadows, hid in plain sight, went unnoticed…

There were secret places even inside the caves. Places that she hadn't explored – both had those tunnels at the back, leading off into some distant heart of the mountain. She and Glenn had given up when the first one seemed to go nowhere, and as far as she knew, no one had bothered to squeeze down the other beyond checking the entrance and first few feet for signs of evidence.

Could that be the thing they were missing?

Was there some place to hide back there?

Tara thought of the killer staying up there on the mountain and waiting until they had been and gone before he escaped, and shuddered. He might have been watching them as they worked. Listening to them as they discussed the investigation, ready to run quietly back to the next antechamber as soon as it was clear they were going to enter the tunnel.

But, then again, if the tunnels led to other places…

Tara turned her head and looked back the way she had just walked. The path between the store Sara Weston had visited and her home took her through a couple of narrower alleyways between other buildings, then down a back road of the town that wasn't as busy. It was an alternative route to going up Main Street, quicker and quieter. A route like that was preferred if you wanted to avoid being noticed.

What if the tunnels were connected somehow and provided an alternative route to the hiking trails, where you were more likely to meet another human?

Tara covered her mouth as the full implications of that hit her. They'd spent so much time exploring the outside of the mountain, looking for clues, wondering how the killer was getting his victims to climb the trails. She had even been asking herself how he could get the older and less fit Sara Weston to follow him to one of the caves that would suit his preferred style.

But if he was taking a different route entirely, one that went *through* the mountain, it would explain everything. How he had gone undetected. How he had slipped away when the camper went up the mountain to find his second victim. Even some of the puzzle of how he was getting his victims up there since the climb was doubtless very different on the inside.

He might have found routes that allowed them to simply walk without needing any climbing skills or equipment at all.

Tara grabbed her phone from her pocket, urgency making her fingers fumble as she missed a few of the buttons she wanted to press. When she had Dorian Ball's number loaded up, she hit the call button, putting it to her ear as she felt herself shake with the enormity of the realization.

"Hello?"

"Mr. Ball," Tara said immediately. "I need to ask you something about the caves."

"Oh, Deputy Sheriff Strong," he said, obviously recognizing her voice. When she first spoke to him earlier that day along with Glenn, Tara had no idea she was going to have to come back to him so many times before the day ended. "Sure, go ahead."

"The two caves we found victims in both had tunnel-like structures at the back," Tara said.

"Yeah, that's fairly common with this mountain. I think most of the caves I've been to up there have some kind of fissure or tunnel leading back into the rock. It's where the water flowed from when there used to be rivers and streams up there."

"I understand that," Tara said. "What I want to know is, could there be a chance that they're connected inside the rock?"

"Yeah, of course," Dorian said. "Like I said, the water flows to carve these channels. It all comes from somewhere within the mountain and flows outward."

"I don't just mean that they might be part of the same flow," Tara clarified. "I mean – would it be possible for someone to climb or walk through those tunnels and reach the caves without leaving the inside of the mountain?"

"Huh." Dorian seemed to think for a moment. "Look, the theory works, but I don't know about the practice. I've never been into cave exploration – I just climb the outside of the mountain. I have no idea if they're even mapped, but I don't think they are."

"Do you know anyone who might know about the caves?" Tara asked. She needed an expert, and she was desperate. If this was the missing piece of the puzzle, it could change everything. If they could break the case tonight, they might be able to save a life.

"Yeah, actually, maybe," Dorian said. "I have a friend who does that kind of thing. He's kind of a renegade – he likes exploring systems that haven't been mapped yet and getting himself into trouble. He probably knows more about the caves than anyone."

"I need his number," Tara said, then added as an afterthought: "And his address, if you know it."

She had another visit to make tonight – and if this was the one who could give them the answers they needed to stop the killer, then she wasn't going to stand on ceremony and wait until the morning.

She needed to see this expert now.

# CHAPTER TWENTY

Tara stood looking up at the door as she waited for Kelvin Day to answer. He was the expert she needed to talk to. He was…

He was not at all what she expected, she thought, as he opened the door and stood there in front of her.

He was tall, first of all, and muscular to a level that she didn't usually see in real life. The kind that was usually reserved for the screen. She was standing on the street, below the step that led up into his house, putting him even higher than she was even in his socks. He wore casual sweatpants and a tank top, as if he hadn't even expected her at all – though she'd called ahead to let him know she was coming.

"Kelvin Day?" she asked, just to be sure.

"That's me," he said, flashing her a grin that was all straight white teeth. "You must be Deputy Sheriff Strong. Come in."

Tara stepped past him into the property and took the obvious route down the hall to where light spilled from another room, letting him close the front door behind her. The open-plan living space and kitchen were comfortably decorated, but the large oak table in the kitchen area was scattered with what looked like hand-drawn maps and printed photographs.

"Dorian Ball said you know a lot about the caves," Tara said over her shoulder as he followed her, wanting to get the conversation started.

"I do," Kelvin nodded. "Probably more than anyone else in Edgar County. Hell, in the state. I'm out there exploring them every day."

Muscular and strong, fit, knows the caves intimately, has a legitimate reason to be out there every day. Tara's breath caught in her throat a little at the thought that Kelvin was an exceptionally good candidate to be the killer. The fact that he was standing in front of her in his own kitchen right now, instead of somewhere up the mountain with Sara Weston, was the only thing that stopped her from stepping outside and calling Glenn for backup.

"How do you manage that?" Tara asked. She glanced around the home; it wasn't a huge building, but it was comfortable and well-furnished. "Do you work?"

"I'm an influencer," Kelvin said, grinning wide. Those teeth seemed to flash light in her direction. No wonder: he was handsome enough, and every item of clothing he was wearing, she now realized, bore a distinctly placed logo. "I film videos inside the cave systems and review caving gear. I get everything I need in there for free, and companies sponsor me to do tough climbs with their stuff as well. I make a decent living."

"I got into the wrong profession," Tara joked. "Alright, so, what I need to know is this. We have two caves which have been sites where the killer has dumped his victims. Is it possible that he walked between them through the tunnels inside the mountain, and that he can get to them the same way through another entrance?"

"Long question, short answer," Kelvin said. "Yes."

Tara stared at him. "Yes?"

"In theory." Kelvin began to sift through maps on the table, bringing out particular ones to sit on the surface. "I haven't mapped those exact caves. Dorian keyed me in on which ones they were. I'm not actually sure if I've been to them before – I only started mapping everything out this year when I realized no one else had ever done it. But there is an extensive cave system under this particular mountain, probably the biggest in the whole range. I don't know for sure if they're interconnected, but if they do have tunnels leading out of them, it could be a fair shout."

"Can you show me what you have mapped so far?" Tara asked.

"Yeah, sure," he said. He tapped one of the pieces of paper. "This one is the east face of the mountain. Anything in red is a cave I haven't gone into yet, just something I pulled from the existing maps of the face. The black caves are ones I've mapped and verified, and these blue lines indicate the passages."

"How do I read this?" Tara asked, turning it this way and that as she took it from his hand. There were a number of symbols she didn't recognize, dotted lines, dashed lines, and other keys.

"These dashed areas mean water-filled passages," Kelvin said, pointing them out for her. "See how the line dips there? What that means is that the cave floor is pretty deep at that point, and the water fills it up to this level. The numbers here relate to the height of the passage where it gets a little tight. These lines mean crawling room only. Any kind of blobs or circles that you see, that's my attempt to accurately depict the location and size of the boulders and rocks inside the tunnel. You can walk around any of those unless there's a hard line behind them, like this one."

"What about up here?" Tara asked, tapping an area of the map where dotted lines seemed to fade out into nothing, not going anywhere.

"That means I looked ahead and I think it goes like that, but beyond there, I didn't climb any further," Kelvin said. "Sometimes I just need to call it a day before I get far enough. Once I identify new access points I can usually get further down, or I can go back again the next day and get further if I'm not making notes and recording the whole time. Anyway, those lines could go anywhere. I don't know what lies beyond."

"Do you mind if I borrow these?"

"Sure," Kelvin shrugged, gathering several more maps together. "I make them digitally, so it's not like these are the only copies. You can take them. You need someone to come into the caves with you?"

Tara shook her head, still engrossed in looking at the maps. There were markings for both caves, but neither of them connected to the tunnel systems Kelvin had mapped out so far. It was promising, though. There were branches of the systems that seemed to be not far from the caves, as if they might potentially link up beyond the reach of the map. "We'll be fine just with these," she said. She wasn't going to put a civilian in danger this time, either – the same thing applied to him as had applied to Dorian Ball. Getting his advice was perfect. For the physical part of things, she needed to take that on herself.

"If you change your mind, just call," Kelvin said. "This would make some amazing content for a livestream."

And there were the magic words that convinced Tara she was never going to call on Kelvin to take her into any cave, anywhere. "Thanks," she told him, not letting her disgust at the idea of turning a manhunt into content show on her face. "We'll be in touch if we need more."

"Anytime," Kelvin nodded as he walked her to the door. Tara got the feeling that he was used to people being more enthusiastic about working with him – perhaps fawning over his good looks, his muscles, and his internet fame. She didn't have the time to cater to his ego. She had a case to solve, and she wanted to do it before the sun rose on another dead body.

And if she was going to do that, she was going to need Glenn by her side. Awkwardness or not, he was truly the only one she trusted to have her back. In any normal circumstance, she wouldn't call anyone else.

The stakes were too high to change her normal procedure now.

Tara stepped outside of Kelvin Day's home, raised a hand in silent farewell to him as she began to walk back along the road, and dialed Glenn's number.

"Tara?" he asked, answering it so quickly she thought he must have been using his phone when she called.

"Glenn," Tara said. "I have a new lead. You haven't gone to bed yet, have you?"

Glenn made a sheepish kind of noise. "I'm still back at the office."

Tara chuckled drily. For once, she was not at all mad that he had disobeyed her orders. "Meet me at the foot of the mountain, near the entrance to that campsite where the guy who found Alec Camron's body was staying. And bring our backpacks. We have a cave system to explore."

***

Tara opened the trunk of her car and spread the maps out along it, using the flat surface inside like a table. Along with the car's interior light, it made a good enough place to check out their route.

"What do these markings mean?" Glenn asked.

Tara chuckled. "Exactly what I asked. We have boulders, boulders that block the route, water-filled passages, unmapped passages, crawling-only passages, and deep plunge pools."

Glenn eyed them warily. "We need to navigate all of that? I don't think we have the right equipment with us."

"No," Tara laughed. "No, I don't think we do. Think about it. We know the killer is taking people and somehow getting them up to the caves without having to carry them through difficult climbs or so on. There's no way he could crawl through tight spaces while carrying someone either, even if they were only unconscious and not dead. He has to bring them with him. I'd say he also needs to be able to just walk with them. No swimming, no crawling – it has to be as uncomplicated as possible."

Glenn nodded slowly. "That makes sense. Otherwise it would be more difficult to coerce them. I'd imagine you could even get people having panic attacks in the tight spaces and causing problems."

"Right," Tara said. "Which means we want slopes that aren't too steep, passageways that are easy to traverse. Walking trails, just like if he was hiking on the outside of the mountain."

"Are there any trails like that inside the mountain itself?" Glenn asked with a furrowed brow.

“I thought it would be pretty uncommon,” Tara said. “But then I looked at these maps. Look, see? There’s a few lines that aren’t blocked by anything at all. It’s like a simple incline. Sometimes steeper, sometimes shallow, but it looks like it would be a simple hike.”

Glenn traced his finger over one of the lines she had tapped. It led towards a few more complex tunnels and lines that Kelvin had evidently branched off to explore, going in a logical fashion from the bottom of the mountain and working his way up. The easy part of the route ended in dotted lines trailing to nothing, where he hadn’t gone any further.

The most interesting thing, though, was where it ended: only a short distance, at least as far as the map was concerned, from the cave where Kimmie Hutson had been found. And above that, maybe another trail away but with no clear indication of anything leading to it, was the cave where they had found Alec Camron.

“This is the one, isn’t it?” Glenn asked, tapping the map thoughtfully.

“It starts right over there,” Tara said, pointing towards the bottom of the mountain. A short walk from where she had parked her car, there was a trail through bushes and trees that she knew would lead to the cave entrance that sparked the whole system. From there, they could walk along the course of Kelvin’s map and see if her theory was correct.

Glenn sighed, taking a moment to roll his shoulders and glance up at the sky. “I suppose it doesn’t make any difference waiting for the morning,” he said, half-muttering as if to himself. “It’s going to be dark in there either way.”

“Are you nervous?” Tara asked. The words came out before she could stop herself. She didn’t want to spook him – and given what he’d told her on the mountain, it felt weird now to ask him intimate or personal questions. Like maybe she was encouraging him to get too close.

“Of course, I’m nervous,” Glenn said. He looked at her in the yellow glow from her car’s interior light. “We’re about to go and face off with a killer inside a subterranean, uncharted tunnel system to stop him from murdering his latest victim.”

Tara couldn’t stop herself breaking into a chuckle. “When you put it like that.”

Glenn looked out at the mountain. “Let’s do it before I get too nervous,” he said, and started to walk towards the trail that led to the cave.

Tara moved hastily, rolling up the maps and shoving them into the side of her backpack, shutting the trunk of the car and locking it. She hurried after him and caught up in the depth of the woods, where the thin path – little more than a rabbit trail – led to the cave. The trees were hushed and still all around them, as if the whole world was holding its breath to watch them go.

"Watch the ground," Tara whispered, pointing her flashlight down at the earth a few paces ahead, her eyes constantly scanning. If there was some kind of physical evidence out here – footprints, particularly – they could help with establishing that the killer had walked this way.

"There's something," Glenn whispered back, his light catching on something to the left of the trail. They approached it cautiously, beams of light flickering over it and casting everything else into what seemed like even deeper shadows.

It was the silvery foil wrapper from what looked like a protein bar. A strange thing to be littered beside such a thin, narrow trail in the middle of the forest.

"I'm getting it," Tara said decisively, grabbing an evidence bag out of her pocket and opening it up. She used the inside of the bag itself to pick up the wrapper without touching it. "With any luck, this has the DNA of our killer on it. Or at least one of his victims, to prove to us that they came this way."

"God, I hope we nail him because he's an asshole who doesn't take his litter home with him," Glenn said vehemently.

Tara smiled at him briefly and then wiped the expression off her face, reminding herself she was supposed to be trying to keep him from reading too much into anything. "Let's keep going," she told him, stowing the evidence bag inside a zippered pocket on her jacket.

They walked towards the mountain, the cliff face looming up at them out of the trees all of a sudden, like a giant, wondering who these intruders were. At its foot, the cave maw beckoned them darkly, wide open and yet almost impenetrable without the feeble light of the flashlights piercing it in the tiniest of spots.

"This is it," Tara said quietly on the threshold, her voice all but swallowed up by the enormity of the natural world around them. Once inside, their voices might echo or ricochet, transformed by the surfaces of the caves and tunnels into something alien and monstrous. Something that might give them away.

"Last chance for second thoughts," Glenn joked, but when he looked at her, his eyes were serious.

"We're going in," Tara said, taking a deep breath and stepping forward.

It only took a few steps for the cave to pick up her footsteps and magnify them, sending an army to march invisibly all around her. Glenn's footsteps joined her own. The beam of her flashlight seemed to show her little of the vast cave entrance, which stretched so far off that the circle of light it emitted looked like nothing more than a pinprick on the far side wall.

But this entrance, for all that it was wide, was shallow. Tara could understand why people didn't come here more often or see it as a tourist destination: at points, the opening was little more than a dip in the natural structure of the mountain, starting wide enough for her to easily stand against it at the top but narrowing to a tiny fissure at the bottom that was useless for anyone to move through.

It was at the center of the cave, parallel to the entrance of the trail and therefore easy to follow, that things changed. Here the cave was wide enough for someone to sit and rest on the ground, catch their breath, and then go about exploring the channels that led in four different directions from the cave itself. One straight ahead, one pointing up and to the left of the first channel, one to the right and pointing down, and one even further right that was also pointing up.

Going further down into the depths of the earth sounded like a nightmare to Tara; she was pleased to know from the maps that the route they wanted to take led left and up. She silently took the lead, indicating as much to Glenn with a wave of her flashlight that drew a pattern on the jagged rock walls.

The path seemed to slope gently at first before picking up a little steam. Tara found it easy to walk up, despite her expectations. The ground was smoother than she had expected with only the occasional larger chunk of rock or ledge that appeared to have broken off and fallen down; she guessed the passage of the river through this way in ages past had left everything smooth, without the rest of the elements from the outside world to change things afterwards.

The biggest variations in the path upwards were the walls around them. At one step they were close, so close Tara thought she should breathe in to pass through; in other places they swooped wide, leaving them a large path where she and Glenn could walk side by side without touching. At points the ceiling was oppressively low overhead, reminding Tara beyond any doubt of the fact that she was inside the earth, and at other times it rose so high that Tara thought she wouldn't be able to touch it even if she stood on Glenn's shoulders.

All the while, they were passing by boulders scattered on the path or small formations of stalagmites, things in the rock that Tara didn't recognize and couldn't name but were most likely veins of minerals or other deposits. The earth was almost supernaturally quiet, save for their footsteps and what sounded like the dripping of water from time to time, even though Tara never felt liquid splash on her skin. The rock was cool around them, seeming to suck all the heat of the day out of the air, replacing it with a cold that was very different from the night outside, somehow damp and drafty, like a grave rather than the night air.

Tara shone the flashlight on her watch as she paused to take a break, wondering. It had been thirty minutes already of stepping silently through the rock of the mountain. Thirty minutes and it had passed like five, with no sense of direction or time in the absence of the sky.

She wanted to turn and talk to Glenn, but she was too afraid. Her own breath rasped in her ears, but not hard; it was simply that there was no other sound to break the silence. She knew that if she spoke, there was no telling how far her voice would travel. It was not just the simple and straight path ahead that they hoped would lead to one of their caves – that was not the only concern. There were also offshoots, tunnels and antechambers and other caves, branching off in all kinds of directions as they climbed through the inside of the mountain. Each of them was marked meticulously on Kelvin's map, showing how he had explored each branching choice that he came to. Tara saw routes that would have plunged them underwater if she followed them, turnoffs that would take them back down into the belly of the mountain only to run up against a cave-in that had blocked the path a long time ago.

And still they climbed steadily up. At the hour mark, Tara rested again for a moment and looked at the map. She handed it to Glenn, using the beam of her flashlight to illuminate it and tap the paper. They were about to step into the unmarked territory of the map.

The climb so far had been easy. Something anyone with walking skills could do. Tara had only really broken a sweat from the sheer pressure of being in a place like this, feeling the earth closing in around you, knowing that you were at the mercy of so many tons of rock. It was nothing like walking on the outside in the baking sun, or in the dark -- worried you were going to fall down the side of the mountain, or having to pull yourself up those broken ledges that led to the second cave.

And now Tara could see – even before it was proven to her that the caves were connected to this tunnel – exactly how their killer could get his victims to where he wanted them to go, push them out there on what must have felt like the edge of the world, kill them, and get away, all without needing to risk exposure on the outer face.

Glenn pointed towards the left, away from a branch of the path that seemed to lead to the right, and Tara nodded silently. They were going up and towards what she reckoned, by the map, to be the surface. If this was where the tunnel connected to their caves, they would find it. She stowed the map away in her backpack, her elbow grazing against rock as she moved. They wouldn't need it anymore. It couldn't tell them anything about where they were going, or what hazards awaited them on the way.

It was not long, perhaps another fifteen or twenty minutes, before Tara started to feel like she recognized something. It was something about the type of the rock, the way it pressed close at both sides, the way it seemed to go on forever into the distance.

And then Tara noticed that the blackness of the cave in the distance was seemingly moving and she realized she was looking at a distant slice of the starry sky, not more rock; she knew without a doubt where she was.

But as she stepped out into a familiar antechamber – one which seemed to come out of nowhere, and matched its sister on the other side of the next part of the tunnel in everything but the opening to the sky – the opportunity to revel in being right was short-lived.

There was someone else in the antechamber.

Tara's gun was in her hand before she even knew it, pointing steadily at the man ahead of her, the flashlight clasped against it to keep her steady. He turned and raised a hand over his face, warding off the light.

"God!" he shouted. "Turn it off!"

"Put your hands in the air!" Tara responded. "Stay still!"

"Is that… Deputy Sheriff Strong?"

Tara paused. She thought she recognized the voice, too. He raised his hands away from his face, squinting and grimacing as he fought to open his eyes in the glare of the light, and she knew him.

Ryan Hutson, the brother of their first victim.

# CHAPTER TWENTY ONE

"Let's go outside," Tara said. Glenn flicked his light in the direction of the tunnel, drawing Ryan's attention. "Slowly. No sudden movements. If you try to run, we will pursue you and I may shoot."

"Jesus," Ryan said. "Alright, I'm going."

He moved through the tiny tunnel one step ahead of Tara, her gun firmly pointed at the back of his head. Glenn followed her; it might have been more sensible to flank him on either side, but given their killer had a propensity for hitting people's heads against the rock until they died, she didn't want to give him a chance to get one last victim under his belt.

"What are you doing here?" Tara asked as they walked. The rock seemed even tighter here than she remembered.

"I'm looking for the killer," Ryan said, as if that should have been obvious. "I told you. If you didn't find him, I would do it myself. I won't let him keep on killing people like he killed my sister."

*My sister*. The phrase floated through Tara's mind. She knew from the statistics that the vast majority of homicides against women were committed by someone the victim knew. Usually a close family member or a lover.

And she remembered something now – something about Kimmie's connection with Dorian Ball. Ryan had admitted that he went along to the climbing lessons with her, which meant he knew Dorian. And Dorian, of course, was the missing link between Kimmie and Alec Camron.

Did that make him the missing link between Ryan and both of the victims, too?

They walked into the cave where Kimmie had been killed, past the stain on the rock floor where her blood had soaked into it. No one had cleaned it up. There was no need to. Yellow police tape fluttered across the entrance of the cave, and the trail that led up here was guarded.

It wasn't supposed to be possible to get up here without going past the guard.

“How did you know about the tunnels?” Tara asked. They stepped outside under the stars; Tara felt the weight of the earth coming off the back of her skull.

“I didn’t,” Ryan said. “I’ve been all over this mountain since Kimmie died, trying to figure it all out. I saw all the deputies climbing everywhere earlier and I tried to join them, but they wouldn’t let me. I found this place and I thought it might lead somewhere, so I followed it here.”

Tara looked at him carefully. There was enough pale moonlight streaming from above them to be able to see his features clearly, washed with silver, even though she now pointed the flashlight down towards the level of his chest. Her gun stayed steady. Did she believe him?

“You managed by sheer coincidence to follow the one correct tunnel that leads all the way to the cave where your sister was murdered, despite never having been to it before?”

Ryan glanced around. “I’ve been here before,” he said. “This is a hiking trail. I used to come here to walk my girlfriend’s dog before we broke up.”

He was familiar with the location. The hint of the break-up could be evidence of an emotional stressor that might push him towards an evolution in his behavior – namely, a violent one. “Did you know about the tunnels here before?”

“No, I told you,” Ryan said. “I never even went into the cave before. We always just walked on past it.”

Tara glanced into the mouth of the cave as if it was going to give her the answers about what the truth was here. It was only black, a darkness so absolute past a few steps that she could have been staring down into an abyss or into the eyes of a killer and not know the difference.

*Someone’s son.*

That was what Lydia Peablossom had called the deputy she saw picking up Sara Weston.

“How long have you and your family lived around here, Ryan?” Tara asked, looking back at him.

Ryan shrugged easily. He was wearing black clothes – all black. Like he didn’t want to be seen. “All my life,” he said. “I was born here. Kimmie, too.”

Lydia had been around Wyatt a long time. Her whole life, too. She was old enough to maybe be around the age of Ryan Hutson’s parents.

She might remember them more than Ryan – she might think of him just as being ‘someone’s son’ that she recognized from around town.

It was all adding up.

Tara stood there and looked at him, at this grieving boy who had lost his sister. He didn’t seem violent – just angry that Kimmie was dead. His grief seemed genuine.

But it all added up, and there was no way Tara could take all of that along with him being found along the secret route that only the killer knew and just let it go.

“We’re going to have to take you into the station, Ryan,” Tara said, reaching for the handcuffs on her belt. “I’m afraid you’re under arrest.”

***

Tara held her nerve, stayed patient and cool on the surface no matter how she was really feeling on the inside, as Ryan sighed heavily and put his hand on the table. The other jerked through the air towards her, palm open, the side of his hand facing down, punctuating his points.

“Look,” he said. “I just wanted to find out where my sister’s killer was. I knew you were all searching that area and I wanted to join in. I figured there was probably another way up through the cave system. That’s how I found the cave. That’s how I knew how to get up there – I just kept going up until I found the exit.”

“But why would you be up there in the dark, wearing black clothing, not telling anyone where you went – if you were there for totally innocent reasons?” Glenn demanded. Unlike Tara, he was starting to lose his cool veneer, starting to sound frustrated and disbelieving.

“I told you already!” Ryan exploded. Out of the three of them, he was the one who was the closest to the edge. If the table hadn’t been bolted to the ground, Tara would have been moving away from it, taking precautions in case it was about to be flipped. “I was looking for the killer!”

“And what would you have done if you found him?” Tara asked, at that crucial moment, knowing that Ryan’s frustration and anger could make him honest.

“Killed him!” Ryan shouted, and all the frustration seemed to spool out of him as he realized what he had said. He slumped back in his chair, his voice going quiet. “I would have killed him for what he did to my sister.”

"Let's take a break," Tara said, gathering the file in front of her and getting up. "We'll start again in twenty minutes. Do you need something to drink? Food?"

Ryan shook his head, then seemed to think better of it. "Water, please."

Tara opened the door and nodded at the deputy who was posted outside – Deputy Stump, who had come back on duty from his home when they called for him. "Water for the suspect, please," she asked him. There was a water cooler right outside the interview room; not exactly a huge risk for him to step the few feet away before delivering it.

Tara led Glenn back to the main office and their desks, sighing as she dropped her files onto the wooden surface. "It's not him," she said.

"It is him," Glenn replied, screwing his face up and shaking his head. "It's all too much. It's not possible for this all to be a coincidence. You said it yourself – he was the link between Kimmie, Dorian Ball, and Alec Camron. He took the climbing lessons. He got a head start on the hobby and then carried on pursuing it himself. He told us that stuff about his girlfriend's dog so he could explain how his DNA might be up there. We caught him red-handed. And that anger on him – you can't deny it. He's ready to kill when you rile him up."

"He's ready to kill the man who killed his sister," Tara argued. "Not just anyone. And not Kimmie. He loved her – you can see that."

"Maybe he's angry with himself for doing it," Glenn said. "He snapped and went too far, and he killed again because he wants to find someone else to blame. Maybe in some kind of psychopathic way, he really does believe that someone else is to blame for Kimmie's death."

"I don't buy it," Tara said. "I think he's telling us the truth. He doesn't want to admit it because he's scared of how deep that anger goes. I think we stopped him committing a crime tonight by catching him out there, but he's not the killer."

"He's the one," Glenn said. "This is him. Case closed. It's over. He's perfect in every way for it."

"In every way but the fact that he says he's innocent," Tara said. She could hear the rebuttal in her head already: that every criminal claimed they were innocent. To head it off, she took a different tack. "Anyway, if he's the killer, then where's Sara Weston?"

"Maybe he killed her already," Glenn said. "Or maybe she's up there on the mountain somewhere and he's waiting for us to release him so he can finish her off. It's cold out there. We have to get him to tell us where she is."

Tara sighed. Glenn made a good point. If Sara Weston was still alive and Ryan really was the killer, they needed to do something. Failing to find her before the morning could mean that she would die in the freezing temperatures anyway – or, if she was high enough up the mountain, there was always the chance of an encounter with their favorite mountain lion.

"Well, in fifteen minutes you can go back in there and try again," Tara said. "We weren't getting anywhere. You need to think about a strategy – how you're going to get him to give you the information you want. It might be better if you empathize with him, rather than yelling."

"Why are you saying 'you' and not 'we?'" Glenn asked.

Tara gestured at her desk. "I don't think he's the killer," she said again. "And if he isn't, then Sara Weston could still be up there with a dangerous man – if he hasn't done the deed already. I need to keep exploring alternate theories."

"Fine," Glenn sighed, dismissing her argument with a wave of his hand. "I'll sit here and think about the interview, and you waste your time."

Tara narrowed her eyes at the back of his head as he moved away; was he being extra snippy with her since they'd faced down that mountain lion, or was it just that the night was getting later and he was tired and frustrated?

She sat down at the chair in front of her own desk, pulling out the three crumpled and half-rolled maps that Kelvin had given her. She spread them out, weighing down the corners with a stapler, her mouse, and other desk items to stop them from curling.

Somewhere in here there was an answer. Somewhere in here was a new location for the next victim. Sara Weston had been taken somewhere – but where?

She sketched a quick line with a pencil, joining up the tunnel they had walked through with the cave where Kimmie had been found. One thing that Ryan had said seemed to not quite fit: he'd said he walked until he found the 'exit' of the tunnel, like there was only one. But Tara remembered, just a few hundred feet back from where they had eventually emerged into familiar territory, there was a turn-off to the right.

A turn-off that wound higher into the mountain, potentially taking them to another part of the rock.

Tara looked at the lines of the trails, the way they wound together. There was no proving it, not sitting here at a desk – but it looked, didn't it, as though the path through the mountain might eventually also join up with the place where Alec Camron was found? Didn't it also seem to be the case?

She had no way of knowing if she was right – only her gut feeling. But she felt that this was the path the killer had taken – the way he had led his victims to their own deaths. She tried to think how he did it. He'd dressed as a deputy, according to Lydia – and that was another stroke in Ryan's favor, because he wasn't dressed that way at all, and there was nothing similar in his pack. Only more protein bars like the shiny foil wrapper they had found glinting at them from the path. Left there by someone who wasn't used to hiding his tracks, who had been careless about shoving evidence back into his pocket and had let it fall.

Their killer wasn't careless. Not when it came to the crime scenes. He'd left no trace of himself behind.

He planned this all out, Tara felt. He knew the secret routes through the caves. If he hadn't managed to run into someone like Kelvin Day all this time – which he couldn't have done, because otherwise Kelvin would have mentioned someone suspicious up there or pointed her in the direction of more potential maps – he had to be careful and cautious. Someone who knew the mountain well enough to be able to not just pick out a cave facing over the town, but also find a route up there that was easy enough for anyone to walk along with being out of the way enough for them to be left alone…

He knew what he was doing. Knew it so well, it scared her. If he was this good, he could keep going for a long time and not get caught. All he would have to do would be to stop killing for a while and he would be able to slip out of their grip, just like that.

Maybe he'd go over and learn the inner workings of the next mountain, stop himself from getting caught over there for a while, and still indulge his murderous habit.

She had to get inside his mind, figure out how he thought.

If she was trying to take an older woman, in middle age and maybe not as spry as his first victim, to a cave, then where would she go?

Tara studied the route they had taken. There was no telling where the trail inside the caves went once it reached the spot where they had found Alec Camron. Maybe that was the peak of this particular route, or maybe it went higher. But it was a long walk to there; maybe tougher the higher you went. It didn't seem to suit the killer's MO to go higher than that. Now that they knew he was taking the easy route, Tara thought that it had to be somewhere that was simple enough to get to.

They hadn't posted anyone to guard the entrance to the trails he was using. Hadn't posted anyone outside the caves where the crimes had already occurred. Did he know that? Or was it too much of a risk for him to go back and check?

If he didn't know, he would go somewhere else. Somewhere he could be cautious. Somewhere no one would know to look for him.

A different route through the mountain.

Tara traced the spidery lines that seemed to go everywhere on Kelvin's maps. They led her to cave-ins, to water that seemed difficult to pass, to steep climbs or squeezed crawls. None of those suited their killer's style. He wouldn't take those difficult routes, and he wouldn't attempt to go up there with a victim alongside him.

It was like trying to complete the mazes that Tara had seen printed in puzzle books as a child: following each of the strands of the cave system to see which were viable. There were no others on the map that showed their two sites so far. Nothing that would make sense for their killer to take.

But that wasn't the only face of the mountain that looked down over the town. From the right vantage point, you could see it anywhere across at least a one hundred and eighty-degree subsection of the mountain's faces.

Tara grabbed the next map and traced her fingers across as many of the lines as she could. This one seemed to end in a lot more cave-ins or blockages; this part of the mountain was clearly less stable, a thought that sent a shiver down her spine. But the third map…

There was a route that seemed clear.

Tara jumped out of her chair and ran over to look at the map they had been using for their search, the one that showed the locations of the caves as they were on the outside of the mountain. There was a match that must be the cave at the end of the system she was looking at. She stared at it for a moment, then compared it to the map on the wall – the map of Edgar County. If the cave she was looking for was on *this* face, and it stood looking in *that* direction, then…

Anyone in that cave would be able to look down across the town of Wyatt, all lit up in the night.

"Glenn," she said urgently.

He looked up from where he was sitting, taking his feet off his desk, and getting up from his chair. "Yeah?"

"I know you don't believe me, but you don't have to," Tara said. "I'm pulling rank. We're going back to the mountain. I think I know where Sara Weston is."

To her surprise, Glenn just nodded. "Alright," he said. "If you're that sure, then I'm right behind you."

Tara grabbed her things from her desk, swooping the maps up in a rattle and crunch of paper, and headed for the door.

She only hoped she hadn't made the connection too late – and that Sara Weston was still alive for them to find.

# CHAPTER TWENTY TWO

He stopped to rest for a minute, pausing for breath. He didn't need it, not really, but it was good to pace yourself inside the mountain. Good to make sure that you had the breath left to run if you had to.

He knew this mountain better than anyone. There was no way they could catch him if they caught up to him in here. He could be gone up one of the tributaries or offshoots of what had once been this mighty river, springing away from them like a phantom, so long as he had enough stamina.

Two lifetimes of exploring the cave systems would do that to you.

This part of the cave was a little steeper than the easy route he had taken Sara Weston, but not by much. It was still a walk, not a climb. Still easy even for someone without any climbing experience.

He started off again, his eyes roving the surface of the ceiling above him, looking for that telltale weakness that he would be able to use. There were certain points in the mountain that were not as strong as the whole. Given decades or centuries, or an earthquake perhaps, they would collapse on their own. They would come down on anyone inside without a moment of warning.

Or they could come down now, and stop anyone who wanted to follow him from using the routes that he knew so well.

It was a shame. Two lifetimes of knowing this place, knowing how it worked, how the earth rose and twisted and left ways for him to enter inside. Now he had to be one of the ones to maim it, to leave it all twisted up in a new way. But it had to be done.

Now that he was inside, they would know how to follow him.

He did what he needed to do and walked away, back in the direction he had come from. He had already made it most of the way back to Sara Weston in her cave when he heard the rumble and felt the shake, and he knew that his work had come to fruition.

No one was going to be following him now.

She was still waiting for him right where he had left her. He had seen to that with the ropes. It was a shame to have to do it this way, to have to hurt her before it was all over, but he hoped the pain would have a sharpening effect on her mind. Would help her to truly understand him. She looked up as he returned from the tunnel, the only movement she could properly make, and he saw the angry fire in her eyes.

"There you are," he said with some satisfaction. "I do apologize for that little diversion. The errand I needed to undertake is done. Now. Shall we begin?"

Her eyes widened and he knew she was afraid. She didn't need to be. Soon, she would understand everything.

He lifted her by the shoulders and dragged her over to the entrance of the cave. Normally he made them sit to look over the town, but she was so tightly tied that it seemed a shame to have to undo the ropes and redo them in some other configuration. She would have to lay down. Besides, with this one, he felt sure the threat towards her family wouldn't be enough. She would end up finding some justification in her poor, broken mind to run, and she would try to get away. She would threaten to come back with them and kill him, like she had already told him so many times. She would really believe that she could do it.

The others hadn't believed. They hadn't been brave enough or sure enough that he wouldn't turn around and kill the ones they loved. After all, he'd been able to get them up here on the mountain, and he was careful always to talk like he wasn't working alone.

"What are you going to do?" she croaked, and he realized that she hadn't even figured out what all this was leading to yet. He supposed there were multiple things you could do to a woman on a mountainside with no one around you in the night.

He didn't think his answer was going to make her feel any better, but she would eventually. She just didn't know it yet.

"Do you know I've been here before?" he asked. This was the beginning of his sermon. He liked to start here. It was true that all new religions required their own guru, their own messiah. They all had stories of connections with God, of holy miracles, of things they themselves had the power to do thanks to angels or aliens or unknown deities. This was his own.

"What?" she asked, her breath high and raspy. She had no idea of what was happening yet – only her own fear. She would learn to live outside of it. She would learn to understand. They had all the time in the world. It was many hours until dawn, and many hours until the police could look for him again. Even after they did, they would find their way blocked. No one else would be coming into his caves tonight or even tomorrow, not if he could stop them.

"I was here before," he said. He liked to stand in the center of the cave and let the rocks carry his words around him, bounce and echo them, give them weight. He loved these kinds of caves with their bubble entrances, their thin and narrow tunnels which did not steal the sound away. "In a previous life."

She did not reply to this. That was fine. Many of them did not. They were stunned at this point – too stunned to answer. The truth of past-life regression was often a shock to people who had never encountered it before, never been open to the truth. Even when they did accept the factual nature of their own reincarnation, they still saw it as some twisted reinforcement of their own religion – never realizing that it was in fact a sign of something deeper.

That was fine. He had the tools to convince them, even if he had to do it one single person at a time.

"I was here in this mountain, on the run from the authorities," he said. It was a tale he knew well, and he settled into his stance for telling it, comfortable and comforting. "I had done bad things. In this past life, I was a bad man. That was what I learned when I looked into my past. Not the past of this life, but the past that had gone before me.

"I learned that I had been in deep need of redemption. I had been so terribly wicked that I barely even knew it. I saw life as mine for the taking, and I took it. Of course, then they came after me, to stop me. As they rightly should have done, in fact; I cop to that. I was a bad man and they had the right to come after me and stop me.

"But being a bad man, I did not see it that way. I ran here. I swore I would fight them to the death if they came for me. I did not know the caves, but I entered them and saw them as a way to hide from those who wanted me dead. I came up here, too high up, found my way through the tunnels to a cave that I thought would be my sanctuary."

Here he paused, as he always did, before declaring in a somber tone: "It was not."

There was a faint whimper or some similar noise from Sara Weston. He could not tell if she was becoming more involved with his story and feared for what came next, or whether she was trying to loosen herself from her bonds and finding it painful. That did not matter, either. This was a journey he was taking her on, and they all resisted it at first. He could deal with that. With derision, with scorn, with disbelief. All gurus who brought the truth down from the mountain could be faced with such things, but he knew he carried the truth and that was enough.

“I froze to death in that cave,” he said. “It was not this cave; I do not wish to freeze to death again, and I know you do not also.” Some humor here, which he always enjoyed. Of course, she would die anyway. It was a simple matter of method. “I should have seen myself returned as a worm or a fly, some low thing that was worth nothing at all but to squirm on the earth and then die. Instead, I was returned as I am before you now – a spiritual guide. I transformed somehow from my hateful life to a wonderful death, and believe me when I say that for many years I could not at all understand this either, just as I know you must not understand it. I could not see what I had done to deserve such a thing.”

Sara Weston made a muffled groaning noise. “Get on with it,” she complained.

He hid a smile, even though she was not facing in the direction to see him. She was trying to keep on a brave front, to pretend that she was bored and not frightened. He was not put off by that. “Do you know what I discovered? Can you imagine?” He paused for a brief moment, but she did not try to answer. “I found that fate had given me another chance. You see, these mountains are a holy place. A place that few know about. Even if you have committed the most irredeemable of sins, even if your soul ought to be tarnished forever, leaving you with no chance to get out of the cycle of endless life in the worst of circumstances – even those spirits can be redeemed here.”

“That’s lucky,” Sara Weston commented sarcastically.

“You are lucky,” he told her with a graceful intonation, smiling as if she were his favorite child, performing even though no one looked at his face. “Tonight, you are going to be redeemed. It’s the only way for you, but I am prepared to do it. I cannot keep all the endless mercy of this place to myself. I must share it with those who are not to be redeemed any other way.”

“What have I done that’s so irredeemable?” Sara Weston said, her tone injured.

“Oh, you do not even know it?” he said. “How like myself in that past life. I will explain it all to you.”

“No,” she said suddenly, seeming to think better of it. “No – first, another question. What if I don’t want to be redeemed?”

He chuckled incredulously. “You don’t wish to return as a better person than you are now?” he asked. “Believe me, dear woman, you might think that now. Your ego might allow you to think that. But in the next life when you are suffering, if you were to look back on this moment and see that you didn't need to go through it all – then you will wish you could come back here and beg me for another chance."

"I doubt that," she retorted. It seemed the view of the city below was doing nothing to quiet or dampen her.

"Remember your sons," he told her harshly, letting his voice crack through the air for a second, reminding her that there were other things at stake than just her own life. Then he softened. She would need more instruction before he continued. "So, onto the matter of your sins. Let me tell them to you, as I have observed them…"

## CHAPTER TWENTY THREE

"What the hell are we going to do now?" Tara asked, staring at the rocks that had apparently slid down the mountainside while they were gone.

"I guess we have to see if there's a way through," Glenn said, ducking his head as he moved his flashlight, as if he could see from here. He walked forward, right up to the largest boulder that had fallen across the entrance to the cave exactly in line with the trail they needed to take.

"There isn't," Tara said bitterly, but she waited for him to finish checking. "Be careful."

"I'm being careful," Glenn said quietly, moving around another few boulders in search of a gap between them. "Just don't shout. Who knows what might set off another landslide."

Tara flicked the beam of her flashlight upwards, looking over the mountainside. There were cracked trees and drag marks across the earth where the rock had slid down from higher above. It didn't look unstable anymore; it was like something had caused it to come down. What, she couldn't imagine.

They were out of their depth in this case if the killer had done this. Somehow, she didn't doubt that he would be able to. The mountain was his domain – his realm. Knowing how to move through it to the best spots was a skill that others were only just mastering. The killer must have lived and breathed this place, climbed here every day, explored it in a deep way that Kelvin, with all his sponsorship and viewership, could never even dream of.

She turned away as Glenn explored, searching the earth and the trees for any sign of something that could help them. A glint of something caught the beam of her flashlight and she squinted ahead. What was that…?

"There's no way through," Glenn concluded, coming out from the tiny nook of the cave entrance that was left, shaking his head. "The weight of the slide must have been too much. Further back, the whole roof of the cave has come down. You can't get to the tunnel at all."

“I think there’s a car here,” Tara said, recognizing now what looked like a glint of chrome. There were branches haphazardly thrown across a shape that had to be a vehicle. In the dark, they had walked by it on their left side and never even noticed it.

Glenn swore in surprise and they moved towards it. It was a car, alright. Tara pushed a thick branch down from the front and found the paintwork sitting under it. It looked like a newer car – not something that had been left here to rot in the trees for decades.

“There are fresh tire marks behind it,” Glenn called quietly from the rear of the vehicle. “There’s a kind of open path back to the road, although it’s not marked. This must be where he parked to bring her here.”

They were on the right path. “Call in the license plate,” she said. She turned back towards the mountain as Glenn made the call, thinking. They couldn’t get into the tunnel the way they had planned, but this was the place they needed to go. It was obvious. There was no way they could be wrong. What were they going to do?

Tara chewed her lip, shining her light down at Kelvin’s map and studying it again as Glenn joined her. “There’s no other way into that part of the cave system that we know of,” she said. “We could probably spend weeks trying to map it out ourselves and find another way through from a different spot.”

“What’s that?” Glenn asked, pointing to a line on the map that was higher up in the same cave system. Before the cave, but way after the cave-in, a spot they would be able to walk from. Unlike the other caves, this one that they were heading towards had the distinct disadvantage of not appearing to be connected to any known walking or climbing routes – it would be far too difficult to get to it from the outside.

A shame, then, that Glenn’s idea was no lead at all. “It’s a straight shaft,” she said. “See how it angles down? There’s no way to use it for climbing. We’d be trapped.”

Glenn looked at the map for what felt like a long time, pressing his hand to his chin. Tara was trying to think about how they could catch the killer another way. How was he planning to come down? It had to be that he knew another route, could go from that cave, and enter a whole different system. They were playing with a deck stacked against them – the killer held all the cards.

“We don’t have to climb it,” Glenn said at length.

Tara looked at him, totally broken out of her chain of thought. “What?”

"We don't have to climb," Glenn said. "Look. Once we catch up to the killer, we can get him in cuffs and subdue him and check on his victim. Whether she's alive or not, we'll probably want emergency air evacuation."

"Are they going to be able to get a helicopter to land near us here?" Tara asked incredulously.

"No," Glenn admitted. "It'll have to be an air ladder situation. One of us will have to help her climb and send the killer up there as well, and climb after them. If she can climb. If she can't, we'll have to winch her up on a stretcher."

Tara breathed out. There was a lot to go through with that statement, not least the idea of sending the killer up a ladder into a helicopter full of air rescue personnel without handcuffs on. That could be dealt with at some later time, however, if they even got there – because she was also concerned about another thing. "It's dark," she pointed out. "And the weather tomorrow could turn out to be anything. They might not even have the ability to get a chopper out to us. Then what do we do?"

Glenn shrugged. "We do our best," he said. "Isn't that what we always try to do? Look, all I know is we're close, and the killer knows it. There's no other reason for there to have been a landslide coincidentally between us leaving the mountain and coming back. He's trying to stop us from following him. Maybe we can even get backup the same way."

Tara looked at the map for a moment. "You want to rappel down into the system and then walk up the way we would have done already."

Glenn nodded. "I think it's the most sensible course of action."

Tara bit her lip. She knew he was right. She even knew that it was the same course of action she would have inevitably come to herself. She had more responsibility than Glenn, a higher level of seniority, and it was up to her to think these things through and consider all possible angles. But when it came down to it, he was right.

If they didn't get in there, they lost the chance to save Sara Weston's life – and assuming the killer knew routes they didn't, they'd lose the chance to catch him. That meant someone else could die later on.

All of which meant that someone was going to have to face great personal risk in order to undertake what could be an incredibly dangerous mission.

"Right," Tara said decisively. "We hike back to the car and grab our climbing gear backpacks. Then we head up the mountain to this crevasse."

Glenn nodded smartly and moved towards the car, back along the trail. Tara followed him a little slower, trying to fix her state of mind. She needed to focus for this. Needed to be sharp as hell and ready.

She pulled out her cell phone and fired off a message to the Sheriff as they got back into a zone with service. From here on in, they were going to be on their own, but they needed someone to know what was going on. If no one knew where to find them, even when the morning came, they were going to be stuck up a mountain with a killer and potentially a dead body. They had a satellite phone in her pack, taken from the station on the way out, but there was no telling what might happen from here on out. Backup was essential.

When Tara reached the car, Glenn was waiting for her. He'd taken their packs out of the trunk and was stuffing things out of his caving backpack into his climbing backpack, making the change. Tara hesitated. What to bring, what not to bring? She wished she was more of an expert. The last thing she wanted was to be so loaded up with equipment that she got stuck in the tunnels, or allow the killer to overpower or outpace her. She stripped everything down to the essential safety items only, repacking it all and getting it hefted onto her back as quickly as she could, knowing that one moment of delay could mean Sara Weston's life.

The hike back to the mountainside and then the climb up above the landslide went quietly. Tara didn't want to risk her voice carrying to the killer somehow, so she kept it to the essentials: warning Glenn when he needed to watch his step, telling him when she planned to change direction.

All too soon, it seemed for her racing heart, they arrived at the gash across the rocky ground that signaled the descent into the earth.

Tara stood above it, looking down. It was little more than a hole in the ground, like a well, just wide enough for one person with all of their gear to rappel down inside. She could see rock, more rock, just the same as everywhere else, but it was a long way down.

A long way to rely on ropes, and a long way to know you weren't going to be able to climb back up.

"Let's get into our gear," Glenn said, grabbing his backpack from his shoulders and setting it down on the ground. He squatted beside it to open it up. Tara moved slower, watching him from the corner of her eye, waiting for the moment that had to come. "Wait… where's my harness gone?" He shoved his hands deeper into the pack, moving things from side to side, searching.

"It's gone," Tara told him. She knew it was gone. She hadn't forgotten. She just hadn't been able to bring herself to tell him back at the car, when there was a chance he might insist on driving somewhere to get more gear and introducing more delays to their rescue mission.

"What do you mean, gone?" Glenn asked. "How are we going to get down there?"

Tara pulled out the harness from her own pack and held it, her eyes telling him the truth. "Kay borrowed yours for the watch tonight," she said. "I'm going down alone."

"What?" Glenn stood up straight, his face incredulous. "No. Tara, it's too dangerous."

"I'll be fine," Tara said, putting the harness around her own shoulders. It hung funny; it was hard to do it up by yourself, especially in the dark and without knowing the equipment to a familiar level. "Can you help me with this?"

"Stop it," Glenn told her. "Give it to me. I'll go down. I'm a better climber than you are."

"No," Tara told him, quite simply. She'd already made up her mind. It was made up before they even walked back to the car. There was no way she was going to let him do this.

Not when she couldn't really tell whether he wanted to go in her place because of a sense that he really was going to be better suited to the job – or because he had feelings for and wanted to protect her.

She couldn't take advantage of him like that.

And when there was already one life on the line, she couldn't let him add his to the list because he was thinking emotionally rather than logically.

"Please," he said, his voice heading towards begging. He was stressed, his face and body language frustrated. "I'm stronger than you are."

Tara drew herself up. "Deputy Grayson," she said, just to make herself even more clear. "Help me put on this harness. You're going to stay up here and watch the rope as I rappel down. If I need to return by this route, you're going to help me climb back up with that same rope. Do you understand me?"

Glenn swallowed hard and nodded. He moved almost automatically to help her with the straps, tightening and fixing, testing, making sure everything was in the right place. They set the rope up together and then it was all ready, and there was nothing to do but start going down.

"Tara," Glenn said, his voice thick with emotion.

"I'll see you when I have the killer in handcuffs," Tara replied, and kicked off the edge, rapidly lowering herself down into the belly of the mountain.

# CHAPTER TWENTY FOUR

Tara's feet hit solid rock and she sagged for a moment, unused to the contrast after the drop through open air. She found her balance again and reached up to unclip herself from the rope, dusting off her hands, and then glancing around.

She didn't want to stand here and have some long, emotional, parting words with Glenn. He was being over the top, anyway. Yes, she was risking her life to go after a killer – but likely no more than she did every day, showing up in uniform and knowing she could be sent anywhere to tackle any kind of criminal.

One side of the route led up, the other led down. Tara knew from the map which way she had to turn. She set off on the slope that led up, sweeping her flashlight beam across the floor as she walked to avoid tripping on unexpected rocks.

The route was likely to be short; they had done most of their climb on the outside of the mountain, and Tara knew that she was close to the cave that she was heading for. She moved cautiously rather than quickly, keeping the thought in her mind that the killer could be anywhere ahead of her.

He could have heard the sound of her coming down into the mountain already and be waiting around any corner.

The thought made her pause, gripping her flashlight tightly, trying to avoid it slipping out of a slippery palm. She didn't want to pull her gun out. If she had it pointed forward in this space, the shock of someone jumping out in front of her would be enough to make her pull the trigger. Even if it turned out it was the victim running away from her captor. Tara couldn't risk that.

She set off walking again, determined not to let fear stop her. She was a Deputy Sheriff – would one day be Sheriff if Braddock ever did retire. She couldn't be afraid. She had to do her job, her duty.

There was a life that needed saving, and she wasn't going to fail Sara Weston.

The sound of a voice made her stop again, listening hard. She was sure she had caught a faint whisper of something –

There! There was a voice, a male voice, floating to her from somewhere. From up ahead. Tara stole forward as quietly as she could, keeping her light pointed at the floor so she wouldn't put a foot down in the wrong place and make a noise, glancing up at every step.

A woman's voice answered the man's and Tara knew in her gut that she had found them.

The sound of conversation made her heart race. Sara was still alive – but in what state? And how long did she have before the killer made the choice to end her life? Tara had no idea how this worked. They had no evidence that indicated a conversation took place before the victims died. She didn't have the blueprint or the map to this.

She crept forward as quietly as she was able; looking up and noticing that she could make out the edges of rocks above the region of the flashlight, she switched the beam off as quietly as she could, stowing it in her belt. Her eyes adjusted to what seemed like total darkness, bringing her more edges of things. There was light. Up ahead, there had to be an exit to the outside world.

Tara was trying to be the quietest she had ever been in her life – regulating her breathing, keeping her footsteps as soft as possible when walking in boots on solid rock, moving carefully and slowly. She reached for her gun and took it from the holster, holding it in one hand but pointing it at the floor so there could be no kneejerk accidents. She didn't want the click of it to draw more attention when she got closer.

As she inched her way through the tunnel, she squeezed her way through a chokepoint in the rock and then looked up; the light was suddenly much brighter. Tara squinted ahead and she thought she could see the sky outside. Compared to daylight it was nothing, but there was moonlight out there that coated everything here with silver light. It hung on the sharpest edges of the rock, giving her something to cling to, a framing for the world around her. She touched the silvery edges with her fingertips as she took each careful step forward, letting them guide her.

The voices were getting clearer. Tara thought she could start to hear proper words – then fragments of sentences, still frustratingly echoey, hard to make out. The closer she got the more she understood. The closer she got, the more she could see ahead.

She almost dropped her gun and ran forward when she made out the silhouette of a woman lying on the floor at the cave's mouth, but she held herself back, knowing that she needed to assess the situation more carefully.

She listened; she could hear him now, figure out what he was saying, even though she was coming in halfway through a conversation and didn't have her bearings completely.

"This is why you must be redeemed," he said, and Sara Weston on the floor scoffed at him.

"But you're not listening," she said. "I'm enjoying the life I have right here. Screw the next life. Screw whoever I am next. She doesn't deserve a good start. She can struggle like the rest of us and try to make the most of it. I'm having fun now."

Were they having some kind of… philosophical discussion?

Now?

"Then it's a good thing for you that I do care about your next life," the man, whoever he was, said, walking forward towards Sara on the ground. Tara could see him now. She was cocooned within the rock, a tight squeeze right before the exit, not enough room to raise her arms. She was going to need to step forward to raise her gun. "The mountain will save you. Your sins will be forgiven, Sara."

"Get the hell away from me," Sara said, and Tara saw him pick up a large rock from the floor behind her and she knew she had to act immediately.

She rushed forward, practically leaping out of the tunnel and into the cave, drawing her gun as she went. But something was wrong. The killer – he had heard her move, heard that first step. He hadn't straightened up with the rock at all but stayed down, swooped, lower, and –

Before Tara could get a bead on his constantly moving body he whirled around on her, holding tied-up Sara Weston in front of him like a full-body shield.

Tara fought for breath and a plan, keeping the gun trained on him. "Let her go," she demanded because there was nothing wrong with trying.

"I don't think so," the man chuckled. He was tall, slim, his arms and legs all sinew outlined in silhouette from the moonlight. "I have her. Make one move and I cut her throat."

There was a glint of something silver and even though her eyes couldn't completely make it out, Tara understood: it was a knife. Of course. He had to be armed with something if he was going to get them to come up here. Even if he liked to kill them a certain way that didn't get blood all over his clothes, it didn't mean he had no other weapons.

If she shot, there was a big chance she'd hit Sara. Even if she didn't, the other chance was that he cut her throat anyway on the way down. He could even stumble backwards, pulling bound and helpless Sara out of the cave's mouth and down the sheer cliff with him.

She had to play this carefully.

She needed a plan B.

And in order to come up with a plan B, she needed time.

"Alright," Tara said, keeping her voice calm and level, like she was talking to a scared animal. She kept looking him right in the eye. She didn't let her eye stray down to the knife – she focused on him. Just like he was a mountain lion. She kept her arm steady, the gun pointed at him, but kept her face open as though the gun wasn't even there. "Let's just take it easy for a moment."

"You managed to climb up and get in the tunnels someplace else?" he asked, nodding at her harness. He gave a wry chuckle. His face was half-hidden behind Sara Weston's head. Tara tried not to look at Sara's face. She knew the woman was scared. She didn't want to risk taking her eyes from the killer. "That's smart. I guess I underestimated you."

Tara saw it – her opening to keep him distracted. "I guess us sinners are good at getting into tunnels like these," she said. The 'us' was deliberate. She wanted to equate herself with Sara, at the very least. She didn't know the killer's story or who he was, but there had to be something there. Maybe he thought of himself as a sinner, too – or maybe he was a saint and he despised everyone else. Either way, he had to be egocentric enough to take the interpretation that suited him the most.

He quirked an eyebrow, taking her bait. "You're a sinner?"

Tara shrugged. "I made a big mistake when I was younger. A big mistake. The kind you don't ever recover from."

He was interested now. His posture was almost relaxed. Even though he still had a grip on Sara's shoulder to hold her up and his knife was still near her throat, he was standing up straighter, looking at Tara more clearly. "What did you do?" he asked.

Tara knew in her gut to play it like a mystery movie. If he wanted to know about the thing she had done wrong so badly, she had to make him wait for it. The longer he waited for the payoff, the more time she had to come up with a way out of this. A way that didn't end with both him and Sara going down the side of the mountain. Tara knew from stomach-churning experience how badly someone could be killed going down that way. "That's what you bring them here for, isn't it?" she asked instead of answering. "I heard you in the tunnel. You know how to redeem sinners."

"I have ways," he said, cocking his head to the side. "How much did you hear?"

"You told her the mountain would save her and redeem her sins for the next life," Tara said. She managed to nod her chin towards Sara without looking away from the man. "Is that really true?"

"It's true," he said. He seemed proud to tell it, puffing up his chest slightly and standing straighter still. Sara would almost be at a point where she would be able to slip away and run – if it wasn't for the fact that she was bound hand and foot. That was something Tara was going to have to work around. Mrs. Weston wasn't going anywhere unless she convinced the killer to let her. "I have been the recipient of a most bounteous knowledge to do with these caves. They're special, you see. Those who die here will be born again in a more beautiful life. A better life. And they will be granted the power to change the lives of others, too."

He was certainly right about that, Tara thought ironically. What he was doing here had changed the lives of a lot of people. "I want that," she said, fast and eagerly, as if he was convincing her of something. "I want that, and I heard what she said. She doesn't. Surely, she's not worthy."

A plan was forming. It was forming very well. Tara just had to figure out how to make sure Mrs. Weston got out of here safe and sound, and she thought that Glenn could probably help with that.

"Those who are the least worthy are the ones who most need my help," the killer said.

*Damn*. He was good. He had his logic all twisted up in the most perfect ways to suit his delusion. "But she said she doesn't want it," Tara said again. "I won't fight you. Put me in her place."

"Why?" he tightened the knife at Mrs. Weston's throat, making Tara's finger twitch towards her trigger. She had to be careful here not to react in a kneejerk way. She had to try to keep control. "So that she can go and you can be a hero?"

"I ought to be a hero, at least once," Tara said. She swallowed. She needed him to believe this. The only way to do that would be to put a little bit of the truth in. "To make up for what I did."

There. The breadcrumb had been thrown down, and he looked hungry for it. "What did you do?" he asked.

She had to tell him now. She had to make it real. "My sister," Tara said. Her voice cracked on the word. She didn't need to fake that. She couldn't have faked it so convincingly.

"What happened to your sister?" His eyes were gleaming now, greedy, feeling that she was about to give him something juicy.

"She went missing," Tara said. Her voice was dry. Her hands shook where she held the gun. "No – it's better to say that she… she almost certainly died. We never found her. It was my fault."

His face was practically shining now. "You were responsible for the death of your sister?"

"I let her go out into the night," Tara said. "I was supposed to stop her. I was her older sister. I was supposed to say something. I didn't. I could have gone with her or even driven her around myself. I didn't. I could have looked for her when she didn't come home that night. I didn't even stay awake to make sure she did. Someone out there found her and my sister died, and it was my fault."

"Did you hate her?" he asked. Tara heard such keenness in his words. He wanted to glory in how awful her story was.

"It was worse than that," Tara said. It was the only time she faltered. She dropped her eyes to the ground and then discovered the strength to raise them and meet his again. "She just annoyed me."

The words almost crushed her. Tara felt the weight of what she had given away to a killer. The weight of what he could use against her.

"This one has committed many sins, but at least she never hurt her family," he said, as if musing aloud. His grip tightened on Mrs. Weston's shoulder as he called her *this one*. "She never did that. The cardinal sin of fratricide."

"So let her go and redeem me," Tara told him. She could send Mrs. Weston down the tunnel, she thought. Glenn was still there waiting for her at the hole in the mountainside she had rappelled down from. He could help her get up and back to safety. "You know how much I need it."

He made a humming sound, musing. Thinking.

A flicker of movement caught Tara's eye and she glanced to the side without being able to stop herself, a reflexive movement no matter how much she wanted to keep her eyes on him. When she saw what it was, her whole body froze.

She put her gaze back onto the killer. Thankfully, he was looking at the roof of the cave, thinking or at least performing the act of thinking, and he had not noticed her momentary lapse.

There was a hand on the ground behind him.

The hand of someone who was climbing up the cliff.

And Tara could have sworn, even at this distance and in the dark, even with only the silver moonlight for confirmation…

She could have sworn that the hand was coming out of an arm that was dressed in Sheriff green.

And if pressed, she would have sworn that out of all the deputies she knew, that arm and hand reminded her the most of one particular person.

Glenn.

Tara's heart thundered in her chest, even louder than before. What was he thinking? The killer would hear something behind him. He would move and look around. He would see Glenn coming and shove him right off the cliff and send him falling to the ground.

She couldn't let him do that.

She had to make a lot of noise, right now, to cover any sound that Glenn might make.

"You know I deserve it more," she said, bursting out in a loud rant that she hoped would not seem too out of character. "What do you think I'm doing up here? I've been trying to find some kind of redemption ever since my sister didn't come home the next morning. Trying to find a way to make up for the fact that I didn't tell anyone I knew where she had gone. Can't you see that I'm trying as hard as I can, and it never makes a bit of difference?"

"Now, hold on and let me think," the killer said, almost crossly, like she had interrupted him in his moment. Tara couldn't stop. She couldn't let him hear and concentrate and know he had to turn around. Her mind was racing. How could Glenn have done this? He had no climbing equipment. No harness. No ropes. They'd used almost all their pitons on the rock face they climbed earlier. What was he doing?

"No, you have to help me," Tara told him. She let emotion pour out of her, raw emotion, the kind that would surround him and dull his senses and leave him unable to respond to anything else. "I can't live with this anymore. It tortures me every day. I was there. I could have helped her. I didn't do anything and now she's gone forever. I chose my whole career and built my whole adult life around trying to get redemption for what I did to her – for what I let some stranger do to her out there by the lake!"

He was staring at her, screwing up his face, moving the knife slightly, not even realizing what he was doing, how he was leaving himself vulnerable…

Everything seemed to happen at once. Glenn got his footing under him and stood up directly behind the killer. The killer turned to look at him, moving his body as he did so, drawing the knife even further away from Mrs. Weston's neck. Mrs. Weston sensed her moment and began to drop towards the floor, apparently deciding that she could try to crawl away.

And Tara's shot became open.

She didn't want to hit Glenn. He was behind the killer but to the right. If she fired and the killer fell backwards, would be take Glenn with him? If she fired but missed, would she hit Glenn? Thoughts and calculations flashed through Tara's mind in a matter of seconds as Glenn took action – the simplest possible action –

He shoved the killer hard, sending him stumbling forward a few steps.

Tara fired her gun.

The shot went where she had intended it to – not to kill him, because she wanted him alive, wanted to interrogate him and find out if there were any more victims – hitting him in the upper arm, below his shoulder, making him drop the knife he was holding. In the aftermath of the ringing echoes of her shot, seeming to reverberate inside Tara's own head with how loud and shocking it was, he let out a growl of pain and frustration that she saw rather than heard.

And he turned on Glenn.

Tara saw it happening in slow motion. The killer bared his teeth as he turned, looking at Glenn who was still on the cliff edge. His leg muscles bunched like he was going to pounce, just like that mountain lion, only this time there was no Jessy with an air horn coming to save them.

There was only Tara.

There was only one thing she could do.

She wasn't going to let Glenn die.

She was at an angle to the killer, standing to his right just like Glenn was, and that worked in her favor. She dropped her gun, knowing it was too dangerous to have it in her hand when she jumped –

And she jumped, doing it at the same time he did, matching him perhaps a millisecond late, managing to collide with him in the air. He was bigger and heavier than she was and she felt the impact like a wall slamming into her, and for a long moment she didn't know where they were going.

Down the cliff?

Into Glenn anyway and all three of them down?

The ground came up too fast and knocked the wind out of her, but in a moment Tara understood where she was: they were out in the mouth of the cave together now, all three of them, just inches away from the edge, and Glenn was still standing somewhere behind her –

she felt that rather than saw it, knew it somehow instinctively – but all three of them were still in danger.

And the killer had so much less to lose than Tara and Glenn did.

He believed, didn't he, that if he died here, he would be saved.

But Tara wanted to live.

He lunged for her like he was going to throw her over the edge or pull her down with him, and Tara launched herself backwards, back into the cave. Glenn was moving with her, behind her, like he was ready to grab her back and engage in a tug of war if the killer got her. He lunged again and Tara was on her back, crawling backwards, kicking out her booted leg towards him and fighting him off as he yanked on her ankle.

He lunged again and Tara thought this was it, he had her – but a moment later she knew she had the leverage to twist, so she did, and he ended up on his back on the rock floor of the cave and she had his arm pinned under her knees. Glenn grabbed the killer's other arm and together they fought him, pinned him, twisted him – until the sound of handcuffs clicking into place resounded through the cave.

"You're under arrest," Glenn panted. "For murder and attempted murder."

"Don't let him go," Tara warned. There was still the cliff. He could still manage to throw himself down it and evade justice. She could barely breathe, the exertion of the climb and the long night and the struggle of taking over, the higher altitude straining her lungs.

She dropped the killer's arm when she saw that Glenn had him. She took a moment to try to capture her breath and then turned to Sara Weston, reaching for the ropes that bound her, reaching to untie her.

"Thank you," Mrs. Weston whispered, and Tara could only nod in response, unable to even drag a word out of her aching and tired body. She lay back on the solid, cold rock for a moment, feeling it under her body, supporting her head.

She knew it had been a close call. She knew without Glenn's help, she wouldn't be here.

Tara lay there on the cold rock and knew she was alive, and in the same moment remembered the pain for the two victims of this killer who were not.

In a moment, she would get up. She would call for assistance on their satellite phone, get a mountain rescue helicopter up here, get them evacuated as the dawn rose over Wyatt below. It would probably be a beautiful and profound moment, one that would become a core memory, a symbol of both the deadliness and the beauty of their mountains.

But for now, she was alive.

She was alive.

# CHAPTER TWENTY FIVE

Tara felt her legs shaking as she stepped out onto solid ground, the helicopter crouched behind her like some kind of giant bug. Sheriff Braddock greeted her with a grin, extending a hand to help her step away. He'd come with four other deputies, all of them ready to make sure that they had their killer in hand.

"Tobin Marshall," she said as she stepped down. "That's his name. He had his ID in his pocket."

The Sheriff nodded smartly. "We'll get him processed and into questioning," he said. "You can relax now. Get some rest. We'll take your statement later this afternoon and get the whole report written up. I want you and Glenn fully rested and recovered before you're on duty again, got that?"

Tara gave him a tired smile. She wasn't sure she had any choice, anyway. She felt like she was about to drop down. Now that the last of the adrenaline was going to filter away, she would probably be asleep within one minute of getting into her home.

The deputies rushed forward to escort Marshall down from the helicopter, leading him away in a group with no chance for him to get free. Glenn helped Sara Weston step down, fine except for the raw red marks on her arms and legs where she had tried to fight free of the ropes he tied her with, and a couple of EMTs who had been standing by hurried over to her assistance. Glenn was the last one to step out, nodding tiredly to the Sheriff.

Tara looked at him and down at herself, feeling like she wanted to laugh. They were both dusty and stained, their uniforms creased and bearing the marks of a whole day and night of climbing, caving, rappelling, and fighting. The Sheriff clasped his hand on Glenn's shoulder as they walked away. Tara couldn't hear them over the sound of the helicopter restarting its engine, blades whirring furiously before it took off into the sky again. By the time she could hear anything, they were all back in the parking lot of the Sheriff's office, standing by their cars.

And someone else was there – someone Tara hadn't expected at all until she rushed out of the Sheriff's office, barreling towards Tara with speed and determination.

"Jessy," Tara said with some surprise, looking up just in time to react as Jessy enveloped her in a fierce and rough embrace.

"The Sheriff called me when they got the SOS over the radio," Jessy said, nodding her head at Sheriff Braddock. "You two were up there on your own?"

Tara nodded. She wasn't sure she had much to say. "We got him," she said, which sounded lame even in her own ears. She felt like she was a kid again and Jessy was about to lecture her.

"You could have called me!" Jessy exploded. "I would have had your back. You know I have more climbing experience than you do!"

There were so many things that Tara couldn't say. That this was her county – her home, not Jessy's. That Jessy had made her superiority something of a competitive sport, and Tara wanted to win just once, or twice. That she didn't think she could call on her sister for this type of thing. That she might have been given a lecture if she did about taking responsibility for her own job. Except, now that she thought about it, she didn't really believe that, and therefore had no real, good excuse for not calling Jessy at all.

Maybe, over the years, she had just come to stop relying on her sister for anything.

"Next time," Tara said with a wry smile, hoping that would be enough.

Jessy nodded, setting her at arm's length again. "Well done, sis," she said. "You did get him. You did it."

And Tara's heart swelled with pride so much that it was painful.

She looked down at the ground and smiled, feeling bashful with how much it inflated her. "Thanks," she said, knowing she had a goofy grin on her face but somehow unable to drag it off again.

"I'm going through a debrief with Sheriff Braddock on the case so I can take the news to my team in the morning," Jessy said, nodding her head in the direction of the doors. "If you're still here when I get out, I can give you a ride home."

"Thanks," Tara said, shaking her head. "I have my car here."

"Alright, then," Sheriff Braddock nodded, clearly sensing that the conversation was over. He gestured to Tara and Glenn. "Both of you, get on home. That's an order. You did great today." With those words he was gone, heading after both Jessy and the group that had taken

Tobin Marshall inside, ready to take over and wrap up the final elements of the case.

"Do you want a ride home from me?" Glenn asked, glancing over at Tara. He knew she was less likely to accept something from her sister, even if she did really need it. "I know you're tired."

"No," Tara said shortly, biting her tongue a second later, in regret at how harsh she sounded.

"Oh," Glenn said. "Okay."

"Glenn," Tara said. She took a breath. His name sounded strange on her tongue. It hadn't changed, and yet it had changed so much.

"What?" he asked, turning back towards her. There was so much hope in him that it was painful.

She thought about that moment. The moment when Tobin Marshall had launched himself forward and for a split-second, she thought Glenn was going over the edge. She thought about how utterly stark her life would be if she hadn't been able to throw herself across the cave and stop him.

About how neither of them needed to have been in that dangerous position at all.

"I can't believe you climbed up that cliff to get to me," she said.

Glenn grinned. "It was fine," he said. "I knew I could do it so long as I was careful. I just had to try and be quiet."

"No," Tara said. She held up a hand and sliced it through the air, like she could cut the smile off his face. "No, I can't believe you disobeyed my orders. I told you to stay at the rappel site for a reason. I needed you to stay safe."

Glenn's expression faltered. "I couldn't leave you in danger—"

"Yes," Tara told him. "You could. I gave you an order. The whole point of that was to ensure that one of us was safe. I almost sent the hostage your way. You wouldn't have been there to help her."

Glenn swallowed hard. "Okay," he said, clearly reevaluating his own actions. "I'm sorry."

Oh, Glenn. He must have thought she would greet him like a hero. Maybe fall into his arms.

But there was one thing Tara knew more than anything. In that moment, thinking she might lose him, it had become so clear to her that it might as well have been written in the sky.

She needed him.

He was her right hand. Her partner. Her Deputy.

And nothing could jeopardize that – not even love.

How would she ever forgive herself if he put himself in danger because of her – and died?

It didn't matter what she felt for him in return.

Cassie's face floated into her mind: a reminder that the people she loved, the people she allowed to love her, tended to get themselves into the kind of trouble they couldn't come back from.

"I'm sorry," she returned and sighed. "Glenn. You're my best friend. I want to keep it that way."

Glenn swallowed and looked at the ground. "Right."

"I need you," she said. "I need you whole and living. Not taking stupid risks because of – because of feelings that shouldn't be there. If you were acting as my Deputy, you wouldn't have climbed that cliff. I can't have you taking these risks."

Glenn nodded, his head heavy. He wouldn't raise his eyes to look at her. "I understand."

No; no, this was all wrong. Was she losing him anyway? Was he going to be able to go back to normal? She was saying it all wrong – making it sound like she didn't care for him at all – when what she really meant was that she cared for him too much to take this leap.

"We have to work together," she entreated him.

He finally looked up and met her eyes, giving her a smile that she thought was brave. There was a shadow of pain in his gaze and then it was gone. "Just like normal," he said. "I take it you're coming in this afternoon, even though the Sheriff said to get some rest?"

"Of course," she nodded.

"See you after lunch," he said, shaking his head with a wry chuckle as he turned to go to his car.

Tara watched him for just a second before she turned back to her own vehicle.

She had her orders. Go home. Rest. Come back and write up a report. Life was simpler that way. And once this case was fully wrapped up, she would feel much better – because she knew a case wasn't ever over until it was truly over.

***

"Oh, Tara!"

Tara turned to see Lindsie Hobbs beckoning to her from the hall. She raised her hand to signal one last farewell to Deputy Collins, who was manning his desk as always, then stepped outside.

"Lindsie," she greeted her. "I was just on my way out on patrol. What's up?"

"It's about that evidence you brought me to be analyzed from the cave," Lindsie said. "Let's walk and talk; I don't want to hold you up too much."

Tara nodded, starting to walk for the exit. Her legs were still a little sore from the climbing and suspect-fighting earlier in the week, but she was feeling much better with a few nights of deep sleep. "Which evidence?" she asked, trying to think back. Had Tobin Marshall been holding things in his pockets when they took him down? No, hadn't that been processed as part of his personal belongings?

"The food wrappers and the clothes," Lindsie said as they stepped out into the parking lot.

Tara's eyebrows lifted. She'd forgotten all about the things she'd brought from the *other* cave. "Did you have time to process those yet?" she asked in some surprise. "I thought you'd be busy with the main evidence items from the case."

"I'd already started on them before you brought Tobin Marshall in," Lindsie said. "I sent everything off to the main lab and I was just waiting for the results. I got them today."

"Oh," Tara said. "Did they have some bearing on the case, then?"

"Kind of," Lindsie said, and hesitated. "Not that case. Look, I actually suggested we should come out here because I thought you might want to hear about it in private – not in front of Tracy."

That got Tara's attention. She stopped walking and turned, facing Lindsie. Tracy was known to be a gossip. Was that why Lindsie wanted to tell her privately? To keep case details from leaking out? "What case was it?" she asked.

And something hit her stomach, a feeling of apprehension that came out of nowhere and gripped her in a tight fist of fear. The look on Lindsie's face…

"The DNA on the clothes came up as a match in the system," she said. "Tara, it was your sister's DNA."

Tara stared at her for a moment of total incomprehension. Her sister. Not Jessy.

She meant Cassie.

"Cassie's DNA?" she whispered, feeling a shiver run through her whole body. It was like the whole world had gone quiet. No birds, no sounds of traffic, no voices.

"Yes," Lindsie told her. "And there's more. There's another DNA profile on the clothing, but it's not a match to anyone in our system."

"Cassie was there," Tara said, her eyes drifting down to the floor and away from Lindsie as she processed what it meant.

Cassie was there. In that cave.

With another person.

The person who had taken her.

They must have hidden in the caves after he took her from the lakeside.

"What can we do?" she asked, snapping her gaze back up to Lindsie.

"I would suggest sending the DNA to the FBI so they can compare it against their database," Lindsie said softly. "I just didn't want to do it without your permission. It's not an open case."

"Do it," Tara said fervently. "Send it today. I'll clear it all. Just send it."

Lindsie nodded agreement and Tara looked away from her again, her mind racing.

Cassie had been up in those caves after she disappeared.

For how long?

Alive?

And where had she gone next?

There was one thing Tara had to know: who the other DNA profile matched.

She needed to know so she could track that person down, grab them by the throat, and squeeze until they told her where her sister was.

And she wasn't going to rest until she found out the answer.

**NOW AVAILABLE!**

**GIRL WITHOUT A TRACE**
**(A Tara Strong Mystery—Book 3)**

**When a B&B owner in a small mountain town is found dead, suspects abound, and it falls to Deputy Sheriff Tara Strong to crack the case. But when another victim shows up, Tara soon realizes this case is far more complex—and shocking—than it seems, and time is running short before this killer strikes again.**

"A brilliant book. I couldn't put it down and I never guessed who the murderer was!"
—Reader review for Only Murder

GIRL WITHOUT A TRACE is book #3 in a new series by #1 bestselling and critically acclaimed mystery and suspense author Rylie Dark, whose books have received over 2,000 five-star reviews and ratings.

Tara Strong has risen to become her county's Deputy Sheriff through her bravery and her brilliant capacity to enter a killer's minds. Small-town life in the mountains, centered around their picturesque lake, should be idyllic. But Tara has already seen enough to know that there is a dark side to everything, that small towns hide secrets, that everyone has something in their past—and that a killer may just be lurking right next door.

Tara remains haunted by her own past, by her missing sister, by her guilt over the unsolved case. She must battle the demons of her own past, while trying to get ahead in a male-dominated police force.

Can Tara keep it together long enough to catch a killer?

A cat-and-mouse thriller with harrowing twists and turns and filled with heart-pounding suspense, the TARA STRONG mystery series offers a fresh twist on the genre as it introduces two brilliant protagonists who will make you fall in love and keep you turning pages late into the night.

Books #4 and #5—GIRL WITHOUT A NAME and GIRL WITHOUT A PRAYER—are also available.

"I loved this thriller, read it in one sitting. Lots of twists and turns and I didn't guess the
culprit at all… Already pre-ordered the second!"
—Reader review for Only Murder

"This book takes off with a bang… An excellent read, and I'm looking forward to the next book!"
—Reader review for SEE HER RUN

"Fantastic book! It was hard to put down. I can't wait to see what happens next!"
—Reader review for SEE HER RUN

"The twists and turns kept coming. Can't wait to read the next book!"
—Reader review for SEE HER RUN

"A must-read if you enjoy action-packed stories with good plots!"
—Reader review for SEE HER RUN

"I really like this author and this series starts with a bang. It will keep you turning the pages till the end of the book and wanting more."
—Reader review for SEE HER RUN

"I can't say enough about this author! How about 'out of this world'! This author is going to go far!"
—Reader review for ONLY MURDER

"I really enjoyed this book… The characters were alive, and the twists and turns were great. It will keep you reading till the end and leave you wanting more."
—Reader review for NO WAY OUT

“This is an author that I highly recommend. Her books will have you begging for more.”
—Reader review for NO WAY OUT

**Rylie Dark**

Bestselling author Rylie Dark is author of the SADIE PRICE FBI SUSPENSE THRILLER series, comprising six books (and counting); of the CARLY SEE FBI SUSPENSE THRILLER series, comprising six books (and counting); of the MIA NORTH FBI SUSPENSE THRILLER series, comprising six books (and counting); of the MORGAN STARK FBI SUSPENSE THRILLER series, comprising five books (and counting); of the HAILEY ROCK FBI SUSPENSE THRILLER series, comprising five books (and counting); of the TARA STRONG MYSTERY series, comprising five books (and counting); and of the ALEX QUINN SUSPENSE THRILLER series, comprising five books (and counting).

An avid reader and lifelong fan of the mystery and thriller genres, Rylie loves to hear from you, so please feel free to visit www.ryliedark.com to learn more and stay in touch.

## BOOKS BY RYLIE DARK

**ALEX QUINN SUSPENSE THRILLER**
FIRST, MURDER (Book #1)
SECOND, DEATH (Book #2)
THIRD, ENVY (Book #3)
FOURTH, LUST (Book #4)
FIFTH, WRATH (Book #5)

**TARA STRONG MYSTERY**
GIRL WITHOUT A CHANCE (Book #1)
GIRL WITHOUT A HOME (Book #2)
GIRL WITHOUT A TRACE (Book #3)
GIRL WITHOUT A NAME (Book #4)
GIRL WITHOUT A PRAYER (Book #5)

**HAILEY ROCK FBI SUSPENSE THRILLER**
BEHIND YOU (Book #1)
BESIDE YOU (Book #2)
AFTER YOU (Book #3)
WATCHING YOU (Book #4)
JUDGING YOU (Book #5)

**SADIE PRICE FBI SUSPENSE THRILLER**
ONLY MURDER (Book #1)
ONLY RAGE (Book #2)
ONLY HIS (Book #3)
ONLY ONCE (Book #4)
ONLY SPITE (Book #5)
ONLY MADNESS (Book #6)

**MIA NORTH FBI SUSPENSE THRILLER**
SEE HER RUN (Book #1)
SEE HER HIDE (Book #2)
SEE HER SCREAM (Book #3)

SEE HER VANISH (Book #4)
SEE HER GONE (Book #5)
SEE HER DEAD (Book #6)

**CARLY SEE FBI SUSPENSE THRILLER**
NO WAY OUT (Book #1)
NO WAY BACK (Book #2)
NO WAY HOME (Book #3)
NO WAY LEFT (Book #4)
NO WAY UP (Book #5)
NO WAY TO DIE (Book #6)

**MORGAN STARK FBI SUSPENSE THRILLER**
TOO LATE (Book #1)
TOO CLOSE (Book #2)
TOO FAR GONE (Book #3)
TOO LOST (Book #4)
TOO BROKEN (Book #5)

Made in the USA
Monee, IL
22 December 2023